PEN & QUIN
INTERNATIONAL AGENTS
OF INTRIGUE

The Mystery of the Painted Book

KS MITCHELL

Print book ISBN: 978-1-7327112-4-2

Library of Congress Cataloging-in-Publication Data
Mitchell, Kimberly, author
The Mystery of the Painted Book
Pen & Quin: International Agents of Intrigue
Ladson, South Carolina: Vinspire Publishing [2019]
LCCN: 2019901366 (print)|ISBN 978-1-7327112-4-2 (pb)|
BISAC: YOUNG ADULT FICTION/MYSTERIES AND DETECTIVE STORIES

For Lindsay
Thanks for always being up for a twin adventure.

1

Pen held her breath and punched the Enter key on her laptop. A notification popped up on the screen. *Your website is now live.* A slow, guilt-ridden smile spread over her face. No boring summer days spent cleaning house for Abuela or wandering Abuelito's dusty museum. It didn't matter that she and Quin had to spend the summer with their grandparents. Pen didn't need to find adventure. Now, adventure would come to them.

Pen read over her own words glowing on the computer screen.

**P and Q,
International Agents of Intrigue**

Are you searching for an archeological wonder?
A stolen painting?
Do you have questions concerning items of antiquity?

Hire P and Q for all your
ancient and modern investigations.

We are now accepting inquiries
for Mexico City.

There. She'd done it. International investigators shouldn't have to be told where to spend the summer by their mother.

"Pen?"

The bathroom door connecting Pen and Quin's rooms creaked open. Her twin brother wandered into the room and flipped the light on. She flinched, shading her eyes from the glare.

"Quintus!" she shouted and rubbed her eyes, trying to adjust.

"Why do you have to sit in the dark like some psycho stalker?" Quin asked. He circumnavigated a pile of t-shirts on the floor. Pen's purple suitcase lay open on her bed, its only contents a soccer ball and Quin's New England Revolution jersey. He picked his jersey up and held it in front of her face.

"This is mine. I've been looking for it all evening while I packed."

Pen pushed the jersey away. "I'm busy."

"You realize we're leaving tomorrow morning, right?" he asked.

Their mother had sent them upstairs after dinner with strict instructions to pack—instructions she had ignored. She would wait until the last minute and force Mamá to realize that sending them to their grandparents for the summer wasn't fair. Not when everyone else in the family got to do what they wanted.

Pen turned from the computer and gave Quin a look that would strip the paint off any of his artwork. "Have I forgotten we're being shipped to Mexico to be babysat all summer? What do you think?"

Her brother pushed her empty purple suitcase off the foot of her bed and sat down. He removed his glasses and polished them, something he always did when he was thinking about what to say. Pen sighed. She shouldn't be angry with Quin. None of this was his fault.

"What are you working on, anyway?" He put his glasses on and leaned over to stare at the laptop screen.

She spun the chair around and faced her twin. His curly

hair—that Mamá complained was too long—stuck up as usual, and their mother's chocolate eyes blinked rapidly behind the black frames. They sat askew on his nose, out of whack from their last soccer game at the end of the school year.

Quin was the goalkeeper for St. Mary's Saints, their school soccer team. He'd grown several inches this year. She hardly let on to how much that irritated her as she'd always been taller than her twin. Pen was a forward and only one of two girls on the team, a fact she was extremely proud of.

She caught sight of the gleaming gold medal pinned to the wall beside her bed. They'd played the championship game only last weekend. Her brother had made a fantastic diving save only seconds from the end of the game to preserve St. Mary's perfect record and win the title. Michael Blalock, the other forward on the team, hugged Pen when the game was over. Her face warmed thinking about that hug. Then she remembered she wouldn't be at soccer camp with Michael this summer. Instead, she'd spend it with her twin brother stuck in their grandparents' old house in Mexico City.

Well, it wouldn't be boring if she had anything to say about it. And she needed Quin on board with her idea. Every good investigator had a partner.

She scooted the chair over and he joined her, squatting down at the desk so he could view the laptop.

Pen examined the webpage again while she waited for her brother's reaction. She'd shamelessly used his artwork to decorate both sides of the page. Vivid drawings of the Parthenon, the Eiffel Tower, the Great Wall, and other famous sites the twins had visited jumped to life. In the center, a black screen held a few bold words in white.

P and Q, International Agents of Intrigue

A textbox for contact information sat beneath the writing. Seconds ticked by, and Quin still hadn't said anything.

"Well?" Pen finally broke the silence. "What do you

think?" She bit her lip, dreading his answer. He sometimes hated her ideas. Okay, most of the time.

"It's fantastic."

She kicked her feet onto the desktop and leaned back, flattered at the admiration in his voice. Then she caught the frown on his face. "But what?"

"But, we can't be international agents. We're twelve."

"So?" she protested. "You know art, I know technology, and we both know a lot about history and archeology and all kinds of stuff."

"Thanks to Kostas."

"Of course." Pen waved this comment away. She was still mad at their Greek tutor for breaking his leg two weeks ago on an archeological dig. That's what caused this whole summer with the abuelos in the first place. Usually, the twins spent their summers with Kostas, following their mother around to her dig sites.

Pen swung her legs off the desk, scattering a stack of books across the room. She ignored them. "I didn't want to include too much information, you know, to avoid—"

"Dad and Archie," Quin added. He collected the books and returned them to the overcrowded desk.

"Exactamente," she said, then realized she'd answered in Spanish. She'd already have to use it all summer.

"Now what?" he asked.

She crisscrossed her legs in the computer chair and rested her chin on her hands. "We wait."

They both stared at the screen as if a request would magically appear with the wave of a wand. Nothing happened.

"Well, someone has to contact us first. They'll probably send an email." She clicked the laptop closed.

Quin nodded, but he gave her a doubtful look. "I'm going to finish packing." He pointed at the empty suitcase and the pile of clothes on her floor. "International investigators or not, we still have to get on a plane to Mexico tomorrow."

"I know." She sighed.

He grabbed his jersey and went back to his room. Pen spun all the way around in her chair and thunked her Sambas on the floor to stop herself. She stared at the laptop, but she didn't open it. Probably, no one would look at the website. No one would hire them. She'd spend the entire summer dusting Abuela's already pristine bookshelves and learning how to make the perfect tortilla.

Pen grabbed some clothes off her floor and threw them into her suitcase. She added her worn copies of her Alex Rider books. If she had nothing else to do, she could read about Alex's adventures again.

But maybe, just maybe, someone in Mexico had a mystery that needed solving. She knew she and Quin were the international agents to do it.

2

The next morning felt like Hurricane Grey Reyes had come ashore overnight. The family whirled through the house, throwing clothes into various suitcases. Maria Grey Reyes was taking the train from Boston to New York to meet her publicist before she started her lecture tour. Adam Grey was dropping the twins off at the airport and spending one last day in the office before leaving for his summer residency at CERN, the European Organization for Nuclear Research. The way he talked about the science institute, you'd think he was going to summer camp instead of an engineering residency.

The twins piled luggage into the back of their father's black Honda.

"I've got paints and brushes in there." Quin pushed Pen's suitcase off his leather valise.

"Watch out for my backpack. My laptop is on top." She shifted his valise away from the suitcase.

"Shotgun," he called and grinned, glad he'd distracted her enough to win the front seat.

"I call window seat on the plane," she shot back.

"Hijos," Mamá called, walking down the sidewalk to the curb, "the last time I'll see you for weeks and you're arguing?" She pulled Quin to her and kissed him on both cheeks. He wished she wouldn't do that. He was twelve and nearly as tall as her.

"Hug your abuelo for me. And listen to her. It is gracious of her to allow you to stay all summer."

"But we don't have to," Pen said. "Archie's only on campus until July and then he can stay with us and we can still go to soccer camp."

"Enough." Mamá shook her head so that her long hair, deep black like her daughter's but as smooth as a shampoo model's, spread around her shoulders. "We've already talked about this, m'ija."

Pen pushed dark hair out of her face and opened her mouth to argue. Quin kicked her shoe just hard enough to distract her. Arguing wouldn't change their parents' minds, and he hated confrontations anyway.

She shot him a dark look and he hoped she wasn't about to have a Penstorm. Sometimes, her temper matched the violence of a hurricane.

"Archelaus is too busy with his studies to watch you," Mamá continued. "And he's too young. He won't turn eighteen until the end of July."

"Lucky Archie," Pen grumbled. Her phone pinged once, and she pulled it out of her pocket. Quin's vibrated silently in his jeans pocket and he tugged it out. Archie. Of course. No one else had texted him all summer.

Their older brother's freshman project at MIT had been a text and location app he called Odyssey. He let the twins download the prototype and they used it to send messages to each other.

"At least this way, I'll know where you are when you're snooping around," Archie said.

The screen flashed alarmingly.

This message will self-destruct in 10, 9, 8w

Quin opened the text before it could disappear.

α: You're late. Why aren't you on the road?

Since his studies with Kostas, Archie had used the Greek letter alpha for his name. He told his younger siblings they could have code names, too. Pen was Pi, of course, since

Penelope started with a P, but Archie liked to joke it was because π was an irrational number. Quin was K, the Greek letter for kappa, since Q didn't exist in the Greek alphabet.

Of course, Archie knew they were still at the house. The locater told him so. Already, a small α pinpointed him on a map. When Quin zoomed in, the α hovered over Archie's dorm at MIT. The phone vibrated in his hands. His sister had already texted back.

π: Don't rub it in

"Hijos, did you hear me?" Mamá asked. "I want you to help your Abuela and not argue with her. Believe me, you won't win."

"Sure, Mamá," Pen muttered. Quin nodded. Their phones pinged again.

α: Chin up. More mysteries than you know in that museum. May be more fun than you think. Have a great summer!

Quin typed back quickly.

K: I'll send you a picture from Abuelito's museum.

His sister rolled her eyes at him. He knew she didn't love the museum as much as he did.

"Are you two texting each other?" Mamá asked. "We're all standing right here. Put the phones away."

Pen's phone dinged again. She almost squealed and shot Quin a triumphant grin.

"What?" he said.

"Penelope Inez," Mamá said. "Put the phone away or I'll take it with me this summer."

She stuck her lip out but tucked the phone into her pocket.

"Mejor," Mamá kissed Pen and patted Quin's cheek again. "Buen viaje y buen verano."

"Ya, Mamá," Pen ducked into the back seat of their dad's Honda. He climbed into the front seat. "What was that about?" he whispered while their parents exchanged a hug. He'd assumed she was texting Archie or one of her friends from St. Mary's. Maybe even Anna, but he hadn't liked that look on her face. It was the same look she had when she scored a goal.

Pen glanced at their parents and mouthed, "Later."

Quin's stomach turned over the cereal he'd eaten for breakfast. Was it a response to the website? So soon? But surely it was a mistake, nothing serious.

"Time to go." Dad slammed the trunk. "We have to wrestle airport traffic." He wiped a hand across his forehead. Adam Grey was not the best driver and traffic made him nervous.

Mamá stuck her head through their father's open window and blew kisses to them. "Nos vemos pronto."

"Have a great time traveling around the world," Pen muttered from the back. Mamá's bright smile dimmed a little.

"We'll see you soon" He echoed his mother's words but in English. He turned around and glared at his twin. Did she have to be such a pain sometimes?

"We'll set up a video chat soon," Dad said. "Maybe we'll even get Archie in on it. The whole family together."

Quin exchanged a look with his sister through the passenger seat mirror. She rolled her eyes and it was easy enough to read the look on her face. How could they be together when everyone was in a different place this summer? Mamá kissed their father goodbye and leaned in one last time, making eye contact with each twin. "You two, listen to your grandparents and mind—"

"—your P's and Q's," the twins chorused. It was a line they'd heard a hundred times.

Mamá smiled. "Yes. Exactamente. But have an adventure too, mis hijos."

Dad started the car and they pulled away from the curb. Quin turned to wave to their mother and their lovely, sprawling old home. A lump formed in his throat, the way it always did when they left home, even when it was for their summer studies with Kostas. He swallowed and turned to Pen. She slumped in the back seat, her feelings on being shipped to Mexico clear. She popped her phone out of her pocket and pushed it to Quin with a warning glance at their father, who hunched over the steering wheel, muttering to himself as they approached the highway and merged into traffic.

Quin took the phone with trembling hands and peered at the screen, his heart thumping like he was about to defend a penalty kick, not read an email.

The words were small, the sentence short, and it sent a chill down his spine.

Subject: Your services

Let's meet. Chapultepec Zoo. 10 a.m. Ma sho.

He read the words twice before Pen tugged the phone out of his hands. It wasn't possible. Someone actually wanted to hire them? Who? To do what? Chapultepec Zoo was in Mexico City, just across the street from Abuelito's museum. Was that a weird coincidence?

The twins were silent for the rest of the trip. When they finally pulled into the airport, their father drove to the drop-off point instead of parking. "Sorry I can't stay to check you in, but I know you two can manage." He rushed around to pull their luggage from the trunk and dump it on the curb. Then he pulled them into a bear hug, squashing Quin's glasses against his face and messing Pen's hair up.

"Dad," they protested at the same time.

He released them and stepped back, his eyes blinking rapidly behind his wire-framed glasses.

"Sorry. See you soon. I won't tell you to stay out of trouble like your mom, but don't make me come down there to bail you out of jail." Adam Grey planted a kiss on top of each twin's head, then loped around the car to the driver's side, missing the guilty looks the two of them exchanged.

"Did you read the message?" Pen asked as their father drove away. She pulled her rolling suitcase away from the curb. "We're supposed to meet our first client tomorrow."

She rolled the suitcase in through the sliding glass door.

"You're not serious about this?" Quin called after her, then rushed to lug his suitcase through before the door slid shut. His twin was already rolling hers smoothly to the check-in kiosk. Why had he insisted on an antique leather valise? Sometimes it was good to be modern, he reminded himself, eying the wheels on his sister's bag enviously.

Pen scanned her passport and pulled up their e-ticket confirmations. "Of course I'm serious." She lowered her voice with a glance at the other travelers. "What else are we supposed to do all summer? Help La Condesa with her fancy parties?"

Quin grinned at the nickname. Abuela liked to claim she was descended from Spanish nobility and "the Countess" fit her perfectly. Abuelito always joked that her attitude was a royal pain, whether her blood was royal or not.

Thinking about his grandfather lifted his spirits. If Pen knew, she would scoff, but he felt a little excited to have the chance to spend more time in the museum, not to mention with Abuelito himself. His grandfather wasn't an artist, but he loved art. He was the only reason Quin felt he was actually a biological descendent of the Grey Reyes family.

"Maybe Abuelito will let us help research a project," he suggested. "Remember at Christmas Abuela said he was becoming obsessed with some book? We could help."

"You are now checked in," the kiosk intoned.

"We're going to the meeting." Pen handed him his boarding pass. "It would be unprofessional not to." She threw her backpack over her shoulder and wheeled her bag toward security.

"We're not professionals," he called after her, but she didn't turn around. Quin sighed deeply and picked up his heavy suitcase. "Right," he said to nobody. "Tomorrow."

3

As soon as the plane took off, Pen started playing one of her math games on her phone. Quin grabbed his backpack and pulled out an oversized book on the history of Mexican art their parents gave them as a going away gift—or bribe, as his sister called it. She stifled a yawn next to him.

"I can't believe you brought that with you. It's so huge and heavy."

She had no interest in art or oversized books. When they'd opened the wrapping, she'd immediately declared they were too old for shared gifts.

"I think it might be interesting," he said, a little too defensively. Pen never realized how her scorn hurt his feelings. Quin turned slowly through the pages, moving from the Olmecs, the first civilization in Mexico, to the Aztecs. The pictures of the Spanish conquistadors on horses battling spear-wielding Aztec warriors fascinated him.

He tried to imagine what it would have been like to see a man wearing silver armor and riding a horse for the first time. Maybe the Aztec belief that the conquistadors were gods was understandable. He started to mention this to Pen, but she stuck her earbuds in and bobbed her head to a beat he couldn't hear. Instead, Quin flipped through the book himself, scanning the pages and getting lost in the pictures of Aztecs, conquistadors, and ancient Aztec artwork. The seatbelt sign dinged overhead, and a flight attendant told them to prepare for landing. He snapped the book shut and kept his thoughts on Aztecs to himself.

In the arrival hall of the Mexico City International airport, a small man in a rumpled gray suit with matching hair and mustache hurried forward and folded the twins into a hug, planting kisses on their cheeks.

"Mis hijos," He sighed, pulling back to look at them. Pen noticed more wrinkles in Abuelito's forehead since their last visit, but his hazel eyes behind his bifocals twinkled as usual. "Cómo les fue en el viaje?"

She pulled her earbuds out. "The trip was fine," she answered in English. This was another thing to annoy her all summer. She didn't mind speaking Latin with Kostas or even a bit of Greek, but Spanish reminded her of her mother, which made her sullen all over again.

"Vengan," Abuelito told them. "I need to stop by the museum on the way home. I hope you don't mind."

"I can't wait." Quin hurried after him.

"Yeah, can't wait," Pen said, but no one was around to catch her sarcasm. Her grandfather was already halfway to the baggage carousel with Quin on his heels. For a diminutive man, he moved quickly. He clapped her brother on the back and laughed at something he said. The two of them looked so chummy already. A flutter of homesickness ran through her. She loved Abuelito, and Abuela was...well, Abuela. But she didn't fit in there the way her twin did. The summer stretched before her like one long siesta.

The old man turned to her. "Vamos, Penelope. Don't you want to get to the museum?" Pen scuffed her feet and dragged her suitcase from the carousel.

"And the internet connection," he added. She brightened, her fingers itching to check the website again. At least they had an assignment—their first as international investigators—and soon, they would know exactly what they were to investigate. She shouldered her bag and hurried after the others into the bright Mexico City sunshine.

Abuelito's museum didn't belong to him. It was the Museo Nacional de Antropología—the National Museum of Anthropology. Quin could get lost inside its many halls while wandering through the ancient history of his grandparents' and Mamá's country.

When he was little, the giant stone heads in one of the exhibits fascinated and terrified him. He imagined the empty-eyed giants opening their mouths and chomping down on him with massive teeth. Tiptoeing through that hall always sent delicious shivers racing down his spine, but he had only to run to Abuelito's cozy office to remember the giant heads were made of stone and his grandfather would keep him safe.

Nearly an hour later, the taxi pulled up in front of the museum after weaving through the overcrowded Mexico City streets.

"Dad would hate this traffic," Pen whispered to Quin. He nodded and pushed sweaty hair off his forehead. The taxi wasn't air-conditioned. They clambered out and lugged their suitcases down the sidewalk leading to the museum. Giant trees shadowed them, and a breeze unstuck their damp shirts. The building was located at the entrance to Chapultepec Park, a former forest that now housed several museums, the zoo, and even an old colonial hacienda once owned by a real countess—the one Abuela claimed as a distant ancestor.

The twins lugged their bags to the end of the path and up the stairs to the entrance. Abuelito waved them past the ticket window and tourists exiting the museum in the late afternoon sunlight. They immediately turned left and ducked into a side hall that led to an even smaller hallway and then to their grandfather's office. Quin loved how it was tucked away like a secret room in a place that already held so many secrets of the past.

The office was un desastre, as Mamá would say. The old

wooden desk was piled so high with papers and files, you couldn't see the antique wood underneath. "What good is owning a desk originally brought over from Spain by the conquistadors if you can't see it?"

Quin could hear Mamá's voice in his head as he surveyed the mess. He wandered over to the small artifacts that decorated the shelves and walls. Some of these were trinkets Mamá sent from her travels to ancient sites. Others were replicas of displays in the museum. He picked up a miniature replica of a stone head Abuelito was using as a paperweight. Not so scary now, he thought, turning the heavy head in his hands. The hollow eyes stared out at him, and he put the paperweight down, facing the eyes away from him.

A phone rang, and his grandfather shuffled through the mountains of paperwork, muttering to himself in Spanish, and emerged with a small, square mobile phone. It buzzed in his hand as it rang again, and he nearly dropped it.

"Abuelito," Pen shouted. "You finally got a mobile phone."

"The museum made me get it," he grumbled. "How do I answer this thing?"

She quickly showed him how to slide the arrow across the screen to answer the call. He shot her a grateful smile.

"Bueno?" he held the phone a few inches away from his ear. She giggled and motioned for him to tuck it closer. Quin felt bad for him. Besides texting with Michael, he didn't use his phone much, either. He spotted a familiar title on the bookshelf.

"Look, it's the book Mamá and Dad gave us."

"Greeeeat. Now we can both have a copy."

He ignored her sarcasm and pulled out the worn volume. His sister shuffled through loose papers on top of Abuelito's desk. He almost told her not to do that and respect their grandfather's privacy, but a drawing caught his eye. He lifted it from the desk.

It was a sketch of an ancient Indian, Aztec probably.

Quin was about to show it to Pen when the museum director's voice grew sharp.

"I told you not to call here again. How did you get this number?"

They both turned to their grandfather. Abuelito leaned hard on his desk, his wrinkles drawn tight across his face and his eyes no longer sparkling. When he saw the twins, he waved at the door.

"Go look around," he whispered. He stepped around the desk and ushered them to the door, his hand pressing the phone to his ear the entire time.

"But Abuelito—" Pen said, but he pushed them gently into the hallway. They heard him say, "I haven't heard from him in two years, just like you." Then the door shut firmly.

"What's that about?" His twin crossed her arms and glared at the door.

He shrugged. "Probably just some art collector or something."

His grandfather's tone bothered him a little, but he decided not to worry his sister. She could spin the smallest idea into a conspiracy and from there, things tended to get out of hand. Like the time she convinced the entire second grade they should stage their own Boston tea party by pouring their milk into the water fountain at lunchtime. Or like this website idea.

Quin bit his lip. He was trying not to think about meeting a stranger tomorrow in a strange place. *Stranger danger*, he thought. It was everything his teachers warned him against at school. His stomach felt like he was still on the airplane bouncing through turbulence.

"Let's explore," he suggested, hoping a walk would take his mind off tomorrow morning's meeting.

"Hmmph," Pen answered, but she followed down the hall. The twins walked back to the entryway and into the large museum courtyard. The building's four hallways made a rectangle around the courtyard and each hallway had doors opening onto the sunlit square. Water fell from a large fountain shaped like a giant umbrella, providing some shade from the strong sunlight.

"What's that?" She pointed to the half-crumpled piece of paper in Quin's hand.

"Oops. It was on Abuelito's desk. I didn't mean to take it."

She took the picture and smoothed out the wrinkles. "Looks like some of those drawings from that book Mamá and Dad gave us."

Quin stared at her, surprised. "You're right. That's exactly what it looks like. I didn't know you even looked at that book."

"You had it open the entire plane ride."

He ignored his sister's tone and peered at the light pencil markings on the paper. "I don't think this is like the drawings in the book. I think it *is* a drawing from my book."

"Our book."

Quin studied the sketch. It was a soldier ready for battle, his shield and spear shaded in pencil. "It's definitely Aztec. See the headdress." He traced the outline of the eagle head that sat on top of the warrior's head. "This is an eagle warrior, the most feared Aztec soldier. That's what the book said, anyway."

"You sound like Kostas." Pen sighed, folded the paper, and tucked it in her jeans pocket. He nearly protested, but he shouldn't have taken the picture from Abuelito's desk, so he let it slide.

"We should be in Greece with Kostas right now," she continued. He heard the wistfulness in his twin's voice. He'd been disappointed that they couldn't travel with Kostas this summer as well, but he didn't see a summer with their grandparents as the punishment his sister thought it was.

Pen whipped out her phone and tapped the screen. "No news from our client." The disappointment in her voice echoed through the empty courtyard.

"Let's go to the Aztec room," Quin suggested. "Maybe we can find more pictures of eagle warriors."

She gave him her 'I'm already bored and we're not even there' face, but said, "Sounds fascinating, bro. Can't wait."

Together, they crossed to the far side of the courtyard. Tour guides herded straggling tourists toward the gift shop and exit. An announcement chimed through the building in Spanish, alerting them that the museum would close shortly. Once inside the hallway, the twins were alone. Their footsteps echoed off the many statues. He felt their unfriendly eyes accusing them of disturbing their rest after a long day of noisy tourists. What if they came alive and pounced on them?

Quin glanced at Pen. She was looking down at her phone, barely watching where she was going and oblivious to the silent watchers around them. Stupid imagination, he thought. Why couldn't he be more like her?

They wandered through the exhibits, examining masks, pottery, and paintings of the arrival of the Spanish conquistadors. Having an archaeologist for a mother meant the twins knew how to examine ancient artifacts thoroughly.

The silence deepened until Quin thought he heard whispers coming from the life-size models of Aztecs in one display. He stared at the half naked bodies and the fierce scowls on the models' faces. Several held spears while others squatted over a stone oven or farmed. Did they know how close they were to disaster? Did they realize the people they thought were gods would kill and enslave them?

"Hey," Pen called, snapping him back to the present. "I just thought of something. What if we get to the meeting tomorrow and our client decides not to hire us because we're kids?"

Quin turned his back on the Aztec models, glad for the distraction. "That seems likely." Good, he thought. Her scheme would come to nothing after all. He glanced back once at the models. Their eyes and scowls mocked him. "Coward," they said. "I don't want to get in trouble," he muttered, half out loud.

"What'd you say?" his sister called. She had her nose pressed to the glass to get a closer look at several clay pots. He cleared his throat and walked away from the Aztecs. Now, he was talking to models. He couldn't tell her that.

"Nothing, just thinking about the meeting tomorrow." He wandered over to a lighted exhibit in the center of the room.

"What do we do?" Pen continued. "I want to get a look at him—our client I mean—but how do we see him without him seeing us? How do we let him know we'll take the job?"

Quin stared at the exhibit in front of him. It was a book—an old one—filled with finely painted figures in bright colors. They looked familiar. "Hey, bring that sketch over."

His twin complied, handing the paper to her brother. He held the notebook paper closer to the thick, brown pages holding the colorful figures. "They look the same," he murmured. He noticed for the first time two letters scrawled at the bottom of the notebook sketch. *FR.*

"What's this?" He pointed the initials out to her. "These aren't Abuelito's initials. His are MR—Miguel Reyes."

Pen shrugged. "Who knows? You're not paying attention. What about tomorrow?"

"Let's just be tourists. The zoo is full of them. The problem will be us recognizing him."

She stared at him. "You're right. Of course. He won't be looking for kids." She typed a message quickly on her phone. "There," she said happily. "I asked him to wear something red and to meet us outside the panda exhibit. It's perfect."

Quin stopped admiring the book and turned to his sister. "Pen, are you sure we should do this?"

"Do what?" Abuelito asked, strolling into the room. The twins exchanged a panicked look.

"Touch this book." She ran a finger down the page. "The paintings are just so beautiful."

Their grandfather stood beside them. "As director, I must say no, but..." He reached out one brown, wrinkled hand and stroked the page gently. "As an admirer, I'll overlook it. Besides, this book is a replica. The real codex is stored in a climate-controlled room in the library."

"Oh, we've studied about codices a little with Kostas," Pen said. "They're always old books, right?"

Quin thought she was more interested in keeping Abuelito talking than hearing the answer.

"Yes, it's a term that covers old manuscripts from many cultures. This, mis hijos, is the Codex Colombino. It's an Aztec painted book. This is the way our people used to record their history—not through words, but paintings like these."

Abuelito reached out and turned a page of the book carefully, revealing a scene of a man wearing a brightly feathered headdress holding a sharp knife over another man. Blood dripped from the knife and from the man's chest.

"That's an Aztec priest. The ancients used to sacrifice the hearts of many victims to appease the gods."

"Gross," Pen said.

"Cool," Quin chimed at the same time. Of course, he'd heard of the Aztecs sacrificing people before, but he'd never seen it painted so vividly.

"When the conquistadors arrived in the 1500s, so did the Spanish priests," Abuelito warmed to one of his favorite subjects. "They eventually ended this practice and unfortunately, burned many of the painted books, although one monk, Bernardino de Sahagún, commissioned native artists to record their history instead of destroying it."

Pen's phone dinged, interrupting him.

"M'ija, must you have that out all the time?"

Quin frowned at his sister, but her eyes were on the screen. "It's only Archie." His phone vibrated, too.

"Lo siento," he apologized and tugged his phone from his pocket.

α: Cómo está el museo?

The message included a tiny map that pinpointed Archie at the MIT library. Quin knew that on Archie's phone, he could see a map of their location with a K and a π on it. Pen typed an answer back before he could.

π: A's giving us a history lesson on the Aztecs.

α: More interesting than differential equations. Talk later?

π: Please!!!

He pushed his phone back into his pocket. Abuelito continued his lecture. Quin leaned so close to the book his glasses were in danger of slipping off his nose.

"This book"—his grandfather pointed to the lighted pages— "is the only one still in Mexico. There are a few others in Europe, the most famous written by Bernardino de Sahagún for the King of Spain. He thought it was vital for the Spanish to understand Aztec culture, but not everyone agreed with him. Most books were burned by other monks. A few found their way into other museums or private collections. Some were lost." He sighed deeply and traced a finger down the page.

Quin noticed the sorrow in Abuelito's eyes. He stared at the brightly colored, oversized pages before them. "Who could lose a book like this?"

The old man shook his head, his brown eyes twin pools of sadness. "That is a mystery I've been trying to solve for many years."

"A mystery?" Pen pointed to the sketch still in her brother's hands. "Is this part of it?"

A flicker of anger crossed Abuelito's face and he snatched the paper away. "Where did you get this?"

Both twins froze. Quin had never heard his quiet grandfather raise his voice before. "I, we," he stuttered, heat creeping up through his neck, "I didn't mean to take it."

"He was looking at it when you kicked us out of your office. We didn't have a chance to put it back."

He felt relieved at her rescue and vaguely annoyed at the same time. Why did he need his sister to stand up for him?

"Of course." The tension drained from Abuelito's face. His eyes sagged more than usual. "Lo siento. You may keep this, if you like. I have other copies."

Wordlessly, Quin took the paper and nodded his thanks.

"Does that drawing have anything to do with your phone call?" Pen asked.

Quin shot his sister a nervous look. Didn't she know when to quit? She wouldn't meet his eyes. Their grandfather cleared his throat and rubbed one hand across his mustache.

"It's late, niños. We should get to la casa or your grandmother will be unhappy. She might send us to our rooms without dinner."

His twin gave a dramatic sigh. "Wouldn't be the first time."

They followed him through the exhibit hallways and across the courtyard. When they reached the fountain, the sound of the water slapping the pavement covered their voices. Quin lifted his eyebrows at Pen. She cocked her head and raised hers. "What?" her eyebrows asked.

He pointed to the sketch in his hands. "A mystery?"

His sister frowned and shrugged. "It's just an old book." She caught up to Abuelito, but Quin hung back. Sometimes, when he looked at art, something about it left him feeling unsettled, though he couldn't say why. Now, he felt the same about his grandfather's reactions to the phone call and the sketch in his hands.

He folded the sketch and put it in his pocket. First Pen and her crazy scheme, and now Abuelito. He felt the way he did when he walked past the giant heads, but this time, nobody was around to reassure him nothing was wrong.

4

The next morning, Pen itched to get to the zoo, but she had La Condesa to deal with first.

Abuela claimed she descended from the Countess of Miravalle, the family that originally owned the land surrounding the museum, park, and neighborhood where Abuelito and Abuela lived. She never tired of telling the twins stories of the old days when Spanish nobility ruled Mexico—or New Spain—and rich families bickered over land, silver mines, marriage, and their large haciendas. Their grandfather always chimed in that those large haciendas were on Aztec land.

La Condesa ran the house like a colonial hacienda, demanding cleanliness, respect, and proper Spanish grammar. When they came for a visit, the twins took every opportunity to escape the house early, before their grandmother could assign them chores for the day.

For their first morning in Mexico, the old lady insisted on cooking chilaquiles for breakfast. Pen's feet tapped the floor, anxious to be finished, but their mother hadn't inherited Abuela's cooking skills and the fried tortillas, eggs, and beans were a welcome break from cold cereal for breakfast.

"Now, niños," she said after piling their plates high a second time, "I thought today you could help me get the house ready for the fiesta we're having Friday night. It's an important fundraiser for the museum."

"We're going to the zoo this morning," Pen said. "I wrote a report on pandas this year in school and I can't wait to see the exhibit after all I learned."

She waggled her eyebrows at Quin and stuffed her mouth full of beans to hide a grin.

"I thought it was all ancient artifacts and old books with you two, just like your Mamá and Abuelo."

Abuela settled her dark, intimidating eyes on them. La Condesa had a knack for sniffing out the truth. The chilaquiles in Pen's stomach danced like a cucaracha. She leveled her grandmother with her best impression of Maria Grey-Reyes, the look that won her mother admittance into even the most guarded ancient sites.

"I want to see that panda exhibit," she said with the sincerity the sisters at St. Mary's would admire. "Today."

Her grandmother returned the measured look and opened her mouth to protest. Then she sighed. "We still have a few days before the fiesta. You may go to the zoo but be home this afternoon for lunch." She picked up their empty plates and gave her grandchildren a rare smile.

The twins rushed from the kitchen and across the indoor courtyard to their room. At home they had their own rooms, but Abuelito and Abuela's old home had none of the sprawling grandeur of the Grey Reyes manor. Instead, its small rooms created a perfect square around an open-air atrium and patio. Crossing the atrium was the quickest route to any room, since every door opened onto the sunfilled area. When it rained, a covered portico allowed you to walk around the square without getting wet. Today, the morning sunshine splashed across Abuela's banana trees and red and yellow dahlias.

Inside their room, the spotless tiled floor shone with light streaming through large, unscreened windows. A breeze fluttered through the white curtains Quin had thrown open. The matching white bedspreads on two neatly made twin beds reflected that same brightness. Their grandmother insisted they make their beds before breakfast. Pen flopped onto her bed and flipped her laptop open quickly. She waited for it to wake up.

"Come on," her brother protested, grabbing his backpack and stuffing things inside. "Before Abuela changes her mind."

"I want to look at the email one more time." Even though she'd sent the message to wear red yesterday, their potential client hadn't responded. One email sat in her inbox. She opened it.

Subject: Red
Look for the matador's cape.

Pen studied these unexpected words, chewing her lip. The matador's cape? She pictured a man wearing the traditional black suit of a matador and waving a cape in the middle of the zoo. Or perhaps she and Quin were the matadors. Did that mean they were waving at something dangerous?

"What is it?" her brother asked. She read the words to him.

He sat down next to her on the bed. "Doesn't the matador kill the bull?"

Pen felt an electric nervousness from head to toe. She shut the laptop and shrugged it off. "At least we know to look for red." But the words had worked their way under her skin like the tip of a matador's sword.

Who could their client be? What job would he have for them?

"Hijos?" Abuela's voice drifted across the courtyard. "Are you still here?"

"Come on." She jumped off the bed. "Sounds like La Condesa just thought of a chore for us to do."

Quin grabbed his backpack and the twins headed for the door. They shouted adios to Abuela and raced down the street to catch a bus to the zoo.

$\mathcal{Q}$

Pen glanced over her shoulder as they entered the wrought iron gates of Chapultepec Zoo. She could see the museum entrance and it comforted her to know Abuelito was nearby.

Tourists swarmed the park, and the twins were quickly ensconced with several families in a guided tour. "Easier to blend in," she whispered. She checked her watch. They had thirty minutes until their meeting, but she wanted to get to the panda exhibit early and watch for their client wearing red.

The walkway wound around the large animal pens, twisting and turning so that it was difficult to see which exhibit was next. The younger children squealed each time they spotted a new animal. Maybe not so inconspicuous, Pen thought. When they reached the giant panda exhibit, the crowd rushed to the fence. Three large bears chewed bamboo and gazed serenely at their admirers.

Quin rifled through his backpack, pulled out his camera, and started snapping photos.

"What are you doing?" she whispered. "We're supposed to be watching for our client."

"Blending in, like you said," he muttered. "Hey, is that a red scarf tied to the fence?"

"What?" She shrieked. Several people glanced their direction and she blushed. "Where?"

He pointed down the fence to where something red fluttered in the breeze. It was far enough from the crowd that anyone walking to retrieve it would clearly stand out.

Pen bit her lip and scanned the people gathered around the exhibit. A large woman in an oversized red t-shirt herded three children away from the panda exhibit. An older man wearing a red baseball cap leaned on the fence. Was he their client? The man didn't look their way and after a moment, he waved a fly away and left the exhibit. The woman in red shouted at her children for poking their fingers through the fence and dragged them down the side-walk. The rest of the zoo's visitors wore shorts and khakis and light-colored clothes.

She checked her watch and felt her heart sink. Ten a.m. and no sign of anyone wearing red but a fence post. Their client obviously didn't want to be seen, but he was probably watching them even now, waiting to see who might go for the scarf.

"I need a distraction," she whispered to Quin. This wasn't the first time she'd asked him to do something like this. She was often late to class and would signal him to distract the teacher while she snuck in. Sometimes, it worked.

"Okay, but you owe me one." He put his camera in his backpack and approached the large woman with three kids. "Excuse me." The woman ignored him. He glanced over his shoulder at Pen. "Go on," she mouthed.

Quin made a face at her and turned back. "Excuse me, but I can't find my mom. Can you help me find her?"

The woman turned to him. "You're lost?" Her voice boomed, and Pen saw him flinch. "Anyone here missing a boy?" the woman shouted. The entire group turned to look at him.

Pen started backing away from the group while all eyes were on her brother. The tour leader, a man in a khaki shirt and droopy black mustache, pushed through. "Lost? You must go to la oficina," he said in choppy English. He pointed in the direction they'd come from.

She forced herself to meander to the scarf, staring through the bars at the pandas as if deeply interested in them. The bears lumbered over, intrigued by what was happening in the crowd. One of the woman's kids started screaming.

"Bears, bears," he shouted, his shrill voice cutting through the crowd. A collective 'ohhh' went up from the group. Pen leaped the last few steps and snatched the scarf from the post. She tucked it into her messenger bag, her hands trembling. What if someone was watching her? She rushed back to the group and straight up to Quin, who was still talking to the tour group leader.

"Miguel, where have you been?" she shouted in Spanish. "Mamá and Papá están furiosos. Why do you always wander away?"

The tour guide frowned. "No Spanish?"

Quin shot her a furious look and shrugged. She grabbed his arm and dragged him away, apologizing to the tour guide.

"Thanks a lot," he whispered. "I've never been so embarrassed. Not even when you took those rocks from the ruins in Pompeii and the police talked to Kostas and made you give them back."

"They were just rocks. Anyway, I've got it, whatever it is." When she'd pulled the scarf from the fence, she thought she glimpsed something tucked within its folds.

"Let's get out of here. That tour guide is watching us."

"You told him you don't speak Spanish?" She couldn't help it. A giggle slipped out.

"Well, I had to improvise," he defended himself. "You never leave me much time to think."

"You're better on your feet than you realize, bro."

They walked to the monkey exhibit, nearly halfway across the zoo, and sat down on a bench. The monkeys screeched at one another and swung through the trees in their enclosure. Pen didn't mind their chatter. She checked to make sure no one was watching before she withdrew the red scarf and laid it on her lap.

She fingered the material. It was light, almost see-through when held up to the sunlight. And something was caught in the scarf's folds. Pen unfolded it, holding her breath. A brown sheet of paper, rolled like an ancient scroll, fell into her lap. Quin snatched it up.

"Hey, No fair. I got the scarf."

"I provided the distraction. You owe me."

She relented and leaned in as he slowly unrolled the paper. A thin scrap of notebook paper fluttered to the ground. Pen put her foot on it before the wind could blow it into the monkey pen, then picked it up. He unrolled the scroll.

"Wow," the twins said together. A brightly colored painting of an Aztec warrior filled the page. The man held a round painted shield and a spear. The eagle's beak on his headdress glowed golden and curved sharply.

"It's like the drawing from Abuelito's office," she said.

Quin pushed the paper into her hands and dug inside his backpack, producing the notebook paper sketch. They held the papers together. The sketch and the painting were nearly identical, but the rich colors of the painting on its dark paper made the Eagle Warrior look even fiercer.

"This is old." He shifted his hands to the edges of the paper.

Pen scanned the painting. Nothing indicated what it was or why their unknown client had left it rolled inside the scarf. She let the painting curl in on itself and opened the note in her hand. Both twins stared at the words.

Find the Codex Cardona and you will be as rich as the Aztecs in gold.

"What's the Codex Cardona?" Quin asked.

She unrolled the brown scroll again and stared into the Eagle Warrior's eyes. "Our assignment."

5

The twins hurried back through the zoo after agreeing they needed to talk to Abuelito. Quin looked over his shoulder constantly. He glimpsed the man in the red hat several times and pointed him out to Pen.

"You're paranoid," she whispered but quickened her pace. They wound back through the animal exhibits, ignoring the penguins, jaguars, and antelope. They missed the turn for the exit and doubled back, anxious to get to the museum. Quin's eyes were on the ground as he thought over the two drawings and what they might mean. He didn't see the woman until he plowed into her. He had the impression of brown wavy hair, suntanned arms, and red high heels as she flew backward.

"Ouch," she cried, landing on her backside. He landed beside her, his backpack thudding to the ground. The woman's leather purse burst open on impact, scattering lipstick, an older model cell phone, a camera, and a few coins onto the ground.

"Quin," Pen protested. "Sorry, my brother is so clumsy." She reached out to pick up the purse, but the woman scrambled to it and snatched it away.

Quin gathered the items. "Sorry." He shoved a double fistful of the woman's belongings at her. She slung the purse back on her shoulder and wobbled to her feet in her heels.

"I wasn't paying attention. It's my fault."

His ears perked up at the woman's accent. She spoke in Spanish, but her heavy accent wasn't Mexican. She shoved the items into her purse and rushed away before he could say anything else.

"That's weird," he said.

"Yeah, she acted like you wanted to steal her purse, not give it back," Pen said. "Who would steal that old phone. You can't even get the internet on it."

"That's not what I meant." They headed for the exit. "Those coins in her purse, they weren't Mexican or American. They were from Spain. And did you hear her accent? Didn't she sound like Professor Flores to you? Maybe she's visiting from—"

His sister gripped his arm hard and pulled him to a stop. "There's red hat guy again," she whispered. He sat on a bench just outside the zoo, scanning a newspaper. The ball cap was pulled so low only his nose and mouth were visible. White hair stuck out around his ears.

Quin thought about the painting in his backpack and trembled. Had this man put it there? Was he following them? "We missed the last turn," he whispered back. "What if he was behind us? He might be waiting for us."

"Just act natural." Pen sauntered through the exit. "Can you believe those pandas?" she squealed. She started rattling off random facts about giant pandas and he tried his best to look interested and keep his heart from jumping out of his chest as they walked past the man. When had she learned so much about pandas? Maybe she had written a report on them after all.

The man in the red hat didn't move. When the twins reached the street and the traffic light changed, they broke into a run. They arrived at the museum out of breath and leaped up the steps. Quin checked over his shoulder once more, but the man in the red hat wasn't there.

The lady selling tickets waved them through with a

smile, and they burst into Abuelito's office like the foam from a shaken-up can of soda. He looked up from his desk, his startled expression shifting to a smile that turned up his gray mustache and lit up his eyes. He shuffled some papers together and tucked them into a file folder.

"Niños, qué sorpresa!" He took off his glasses and laid them on top of the folder. "But to what do I owe this pleasure? La Condesa said she allowed you to visit the zoo today."

"We got bored with the animals," Pen said. "And they stank."

The old man chuckled. "Well, that is one good thing about working with art and artifacts. They don't smell like monkeys...usually."

Quin shifted his backpack so he could pull out the sketch their grandfather had given them. He and Pen had agreed not to show the painting from the red scarf to their grandfather just yet. He pushed the sketch onto the desk.

"Abuelito, can you tell us more about the codexes you talked about yesterday? We decided that was more interesting than animals."

Their grandfather took the paper and nodded. "Of course. You are your mother's children. And your grandfather's," he added with a wink. "First, the word codex is *codices* in plural, in case you want to talk about this around your grandmother. You know how she is with grammar."

"Ay." She put a hand to her forehead in a gesture that mimicked Abuela when she heard incorrect grammar, which was nearly all the time when Pen spoke Spanish.

Abuelito nodded. "Exactamente. But of course, a codex *is* a book, and in this case", he pointed to the sketch, "a book painted by Aztec scribes and commissioned by the King of Spain so he could learn of life here in New Spain."

"Are there many books?" she asked. "Are they all called codex? You said yesterday most of them were in Europe, not Mexico."

Quin perched beside his twin on the edge of one of two

chairs in front of the desk. He knew what Pen was trying to do. How could they ask Abuelito about the Codex Cardona without him guessing they had a secret?

"Alas, yes, but we do have the Codex Colombino here." Their grandfather put his glasses back on. "You saw it yesterday. When I was a younger man and traveled more often for the museum, I was privileged to see several other painted books." His hand rested lightly on top of the folder on his desk and he got a faraway look in his eyes. "Looking for codices was sort of a hobby for me and a friend of mine. We spent several summer breaks and vacations trying to find clues to long forgotten books."

"Like a treasure hunt," Quin said.

"Sí," Abuelito said with a smile.

"You don't still look for them?" Pen asked.

He frowned and traced the pencil lines on the sketch before clearing his throat. "Your grandmother asked me to stop looking into the painted books a few years ago."

"I thought Abuela liked art," Pen said. "She's always having those parties."

A small smile crossed Abuelito's face. "Fundraisers," he corrected. "And she does, but she felt I'd become obsessed with a certain codex and she was concerned."

He removed his glasses and rubbed his eyes with one hand.

Quin shot Pen a nervous look. His grandfather's tone made him uneasy. If he liked painted books so much, he probably knew about the Codex Cardona, but it was obvious their client wanted to keep himself secret, and Quin didn't relish the thought of explaining their website to Abuelito, either. He stared at the stone head on the desk. Its brows were furrowed in disapproval. He turned away. *We're not doing anything wrong by not telling Abuelito about the Eagle Warrior,* he thought. *We're just asking questions.*

The speaker on the desk phone buzzed. "Señor Reyes, your appointment is here," the secretary's voice intoned.

The old man sighed and put his glasses back on. He slid the folder into a desk drawer and stood. "If you want to know more about codices, my secretary can take you to the museum library. It's normally off limits for anyone but employees and scholars but," he patted Quin on the shoulder and laid a wrinkled hand on Pen's head, "you are both nothing if not accomplished scholars already, thanks to your mother and, of course, to Kostas."

"Wow, gracias," Pen said.

"De nada," he said. "I'll take you to her quickly."

She followed Abuelito out of the office. Quin shouldered his backpack. His gaze fell on the head one more time. Its empty eyes glared at him, ancient and disapproving.

"Shut up," he said. He shook his head, glad his sister had already left before she heard him talking to a miniature stone head.

6

Several hours later, Pen's stomach growled so loudly the grad student several tables over looked up and frowned. She put her head on the table and sighed. Her empty stomach still hadn't adjusted from the eleven o'clock school lunch schedule. To make matters worse, she and Quin had flipped through all the books Abuelito's secretary found on Mexican painted books and found no mention of the Codex Cardona anywhere.

"Anything?" she mumbled at her brother, not lifting her head. He had pulled his glasses off and his nose nearly touched the pages. He rubbed his eyes and slammed the book shut. The grad student made rude noises and glared at them as he gathered up his papers and stormed out of the room.

"Finally, some privacy." Pen sighed. "But why can't we—"

"How's it going?" Abuelito's secretary called out as she breezed into the room. "Any luck on your research?" She gave the children an indulgent smile. Pen could tell the woman thought it was cute they were playing at research—only they weren't playing. She narrowed her eyes at the secretary, but Quin spoke up, giving her a slight shake of his head as he did so.

"We can't seem to find any information on a certain

codex. It's not famous so these books don't mention it."

"Hmm. Your grandfather might know, but he's still in his meeting." She scooped up several books and set them on a cart to be re-shelved.

"We can't ask Abuelito," Pen whispered. She slumped in her chair. Was their search ending so soon?

"I know." The secretary paused as she picked up the last book. "You could ask around the antique bookshops—the ones that sell the older works. I know one shop in particular your grandfather has visited nearly every week for the last two years. I can give you the address."

Quin checked his watch. "We can't. La Con...I mean Abuela," he amended in front of the secretary, "expects us back for lunch. We're already late."

"Oh, I forgot to tell you your grandmother called to say she had some emergency with the party for Friday she had to take care of. She apologized and said she would see you later this evening."

The secretary reached into her pocket and drew out some pesos. "Your grandfather asked me to give you this. He said there are lunch carts in the park and you two should enjoy yourselves this afternoon before your grandmother puts you to work." She handed the colorful pesos to Quin and he shoved them into his pocket.

Pen shot him a quick smile. "I guess we can go to the bookshop after all."

They stopped at the secretary's desk to get the address. Abuelito's door remained shut and the twins decided it was better not to interrupt his meeting to tell him where they were going. "He might want to go with us," Pen said.

"He might not want us to go at all," Quin said. "This bookstore is all the way downtown. We'll have to hurry if we want to get there and back before Abuela knows how long we've been gone."

They left the museum's cool interior for the warm afternoon sunshine. Pen shaded her eyes. Mexico City's sunlight was so much stronger than Boston's. Maybe that had to do with being over 7,000 feet in altitude. The sun actually was closer.

The rich smell of frying meat and fresh tortillas filled the air. "Mmm. Do we have time for tacos?" Quin stopped walking and stared at the row of taco stands in front of the museum.

Her stomach rumbled in response and she realized she might not make it to the bookstore if she didn't put something in it. "Maybe one or two."

Four tacos later, the twins stood in front of Librería Madero. No cars or buses were allowed on this downtown street. Pedestrians brushed past them on their way to or from the historic district of Mexico City. Pen felt comfortable in the crowd. Anonymous, unlike their encounter at the zoo that morning.

Her phone dinged. She slipped it out of her pocket.

α: Field trip?

"Oops. I forgot about Archie. He knows where we are."

Quin shrugged. "So what? He's in Boston. Say hi for me."

When she looked down, the message had already disappeared. She opened Odyssey and typed.

π: Sort of. K says hi.

She paused, then typed, *TTYL*. She didn't even check to see where Archie was. Instead, Pen turned the phone to silent, something she never did. But being an international agent was serious business.

"Well, let's go in." A bell jangled as they walked inside. She stopped, and her brother bumped into her.

"Hey, why'd you stop?"

Pen closed her eyes and breathed deeply. "It smells like heaven."

The scent of old books permeated the air. Sunshine slanted through the windows and exposed golden flecks of dust dancing in the rays. Dark wooden shelves lined every wall of the store and filled most of the floor as well. The bookshelves were twice as tall as the twins and packed with books of every size, many of them faded with age. Other antiquities were scattered throughout the store as well. Pen noticed an old cash register and a glass-covered counter containing old coins and Mexican jewelry. Quin stepped away from her to examine some paintings on the wall behind the register.

She stretched out her hand and brushed the spines of books on the first shelf. The leather was cracked on some spines and when she withdrew a book and opened it, the paper was stained and spotted with decay. "These books aren't as old as they look," she said to her twin, not realizing he'd wandered to the far end of the store.

"Tienes razón," a voice said. "But how is it a young girl is right about my books?" An older man stepped out from the other side of the book shelf, startling her so that she almost dropped the book. The man had a brown beard merging into grey and wore gold-rimmed glasses and an English tweed cap. He plucked the book from her hand and held it close to his substantial stomach while examining her over the lenses of his glasses. "Y? Tell me."

Pen didn't like the way he'd taken the book away as if her hands hadn't been washed for hours, although they hadn't. She also didn't like the way his nose turned up and the little bump on the end of it. La Condesa always said people couldn't help the way they looked, but they could adjust their appearance—a jab at Pen's often unkempt hair, she suspected. Well maybe this man couldn't help his nose, but he could help being rude.

"It's obvious." She adopted the voice she used for school reports, a deliberate copy of her mother's lecturing tone. "Books break down because of the amount of acid contained in the wood pulp used to make paper. Most books printed on wood pulp paper were made in the nineteenth and twentieth centuries."

She gestured to the shelves around them. "These books are breaking down, which means they're no older than the 1800s." She sniffed like she'd seen Abuela do when she was unimpressed by an art dealer. "Though I doubt they're older than 1950. They're just in poor condition."

The man regarded her with something like admiration in his eyes, coupled with annoyance. Well, she was used to that. She felt someone approach behind her. Quin whispered, "What's going on?"

"So, you children know a little something about old books. You are right in saying these books are not too old. I keep them up front for the tourists. The real treasures are in the back."

Her brother nodded. "He's right. I already found them."

Pen deflated a little. "Well, at least you have older books."

The man snorted and gestured for them to follow. Worn rugs muffled their steps as they weaved through shelves to the back of the store. He held a finger in the air and ran it down a shelf, keeping his finger an inch away from the spines. After deliberating a moment, he carefully pulled a thick book from the shelf and proffered it to her. She reached for it, but he stepped back with a shake of his head. Pen glowered but read the title in Spanish. *The History of Don Quixote.*

She recognized the title. They'd read it with Kostas two summers ago. She had found the story about an old man pretending to be a knight pretty silly.

"That is an original." The man placed the book carefully back on the shelf. "This has been a fascinating diversion, but I don't usually sell to children and," he surveyed their jeans and t-shirts, "I'm certain you're not here to buy."

"We're visiting our grandfather." Quin jumped into the conversation. "This is his favorite bookshop."

The bookseller's stern features softened slightly. "Ah. And who is your abuelo?"

"Miguel Reyes de la Cruz," the twins said together. They

grinned at each other and Quin managed to pinch her before she could jinx him.

The bookseller slapped his forehead. "Of course. El director del museo. Why didn't you say so? Are you here to pick up his package?"

The twins shared a look of surprise, but Pen recovered first. After all, investigators had to adjust quickly to new developments.

"Yes. Abuelito sent us. He has a meeting all afternoon."

The bookseller frowned at them and rubbed his hands together. "To tell you the truth, I'm a little surprised he would send his grandchildren. Maybe I should call—"

The doorbell jingled, and the man peered past the shelves. "Un minuto, niños." The bookseller walked to the front of the store.

"What package are we picking up?" Quin whispered.

Pen shrugged. "I don't know. But as long as we're here, we might as well. And maybe he can tell us something about painted books, too."

He checked his watch. "We need to hurry."

She nodded and motioned him forward. Together, they walked to the front, the conversation between the bookseller and customer becoming clear.

"An unusual request. I have only replicas of these painted books, nothing authentic."

"But this one may come to you only in pages, not as a whole book," a man said. His voice was smooth and the S's on the end of his words slid out like a hissing snake. "If it came to your shop, you might recognize it only by the uniqueness of its paintings-s-s. Like nothing you have s-s-seen from the time."

Quin frowned and poked Pen in the back. She shushed him, her eyes wide and brows furrowed, conveying both her annoyance and her brother's alarm at the same time. She knew this voice, but from where?

"If you want to leave your information, I will keep my eyes open for this book—or pages," the bookseller said.

"But I have reliable information that you have, in fact, come into contact with these pages," the man continued.

"Lo siento, but you're mistaken," the bookseller apologized. He sounded anything but sorry.

The speaker was Spanish, Pen was certain of that. His accent gave him away, but the twins had spent little time in Spain. A quick family trip one summer after spending most of their time with Kostas in Italy. Why would she know this man?

It hit the twins at the same time. She whirled around just as Quin reached out to grab her arm. Her shoulder banged into his outstretched hand and knocked it into a bookshelf. His knuckles struck the hard wood with the sting of an old-fashioned rapping. "Ouch," he yelped, sticking his knuckles in his mouth.

"Sorry," she said. "It's him."

He pulled his knuckles away. "I know—" He broke off and his face tightened. Slowly, Pen turned around. A tall man with long black hair pulled neatly back and sallow skin the color of an old book peered over the shelf at them.

The twins shared a look of misery. "Hello, Professor Flores," they mumbled.

The man at the counter surveyed them, his thin lips turning down like he'd just sucked on a lime. "Penelope and Quintus Grey Reyes, does your grandfather know you are here?"

7

The twins spent most summers traveling between ancient sites and universities, often following their mother's dig schedule. They met many of Maria Grey-Reyes' colleagues through these trips. The best, of course, was Kostas. The worst was Professor Flores.

Quin surveyed the Spanish professor's long, oily pony-tail and nearly gagged. Everything about him was greasy, from his hair and skin to his manner of speaking. The last time they'd seen him was during their family trip to Spain two years ago. The professor insisted on having them over for dinner, a long boring affair made bearable only by the many original paintings hanging in his Madrid apartment. The dinner lasted well past midnight and ended when Professor Flores tried to kiss their mother good night. Their father stepped in and declared the evening over. Quin remembered his father's indignation as they hustled into a taxi.

"What did you ever see in that slickster?" Adam Grey exclaimed.

Their mother laughed. "Oh, he was quite the catch at university. Todas las chicas fell over themselves trying to get a date with handsome Jose Luis."

"Every girl but you," Adam Grey said. He leaned over and got the good night kiss Professor Flores had tried to steal, and Quin felt extraordinarily happy his mother hadn't fallen for the man and had married their father instead.

"What are you doing here?" Pen demanded, bringing him back to the present. He narrowed his eyes at the professor, remembering how he'd tried to steal a kiss from Mamá.

They stood at the front of the bookstore near the antique cash register. The professor leaned casually against the counter and the bookseller frowned at the streak his elbow left.

"Didn't your mother tell you? I told her I wanted to visit your grandfather's museum and that I would, how do you say it, check you." He bared his teeth at them, which Quin supposed was his version of a smile.

"Check up," Pen muttered. The professor gave her a forced smile.

"Yes, of course."

The bookseller held a slim manila envelope in his hands and he motioned to the children. "Your grandfather's package." He handed it to Quin. "Handle it carefully. Tell your grandfather to call me if he has questions."

"We will." He itched to open the envelope and peer inside, but Professor Flores was looking at the envelope like it was a plate of tacos he wanted to devour. Quin clutched the envelope with one hand and pointed to a painting of a brightly feathered quetzal bird on the wall behind the cash register.

"Is that old, too?"

The bookseller waved the question away. "No, it's a knock-off of the old Aztec paintings. I sell them to tourists."

"I'm surprised you can't see the difference between fine art and cheap imitation, Quintus." Professor Flores looked down his nose at the painting. "I thought you considered yourself an artist."

He flushed and clamped his mouth shut. Actually, Professor Flores was correct. The lines were sloppily drawn, and the color not even filled in in places. He should have noticed that.

"It reminds me of the paintings in the codices," Pen said. Professor Flores gave her a sharp look.

"What could you possibly know about painted books?"

"The girl knows more about books than you think," the bookseller said.

"Enough to know not every codex is in a museum," she retorted. Quin elbowed her. When would she learn to bite her tongue?

The professor's nostrils flared, and his lips pressed into the thin line of a pencil. "You were eavesdropping on my conversation. Didn't your mother ever tell you that's rude?"

"Our mother has told us lots of things, starting with why she never dated you," she retorted. Quin slowly shook his head at her, his eyes begging her not to say another word.

Twin streaks of pink crept up the professor's face. He straightened the collar of his white shirt and smoothed the chest hairs peeking out from the unbuttoned top. "Perhaps I will discuss your behavior with your grandparents at the fiesta. They might be interested to know how impolitely their grandchildren are behaving."

Pen shot back. "I think they'll be too busy discussing art. Isn't that why you're here? Or are you looking for something else in Mexico?"

Professor Flores' black eyes smoldered. He stepped forward and Quin put a hand on his sister's arm, ready to pull her away. The last thing he wanted was a confrontation.

"You're more like your mother every day, Penelope," the man finally said. "Please tell your grandparents I'm looking forward to their hospitality." He turned to the bookseller and handed him a stained business card. "Inform me if you come across what we discussed, and I will make sure it is worth your time and trouble." He left the shop without saying goodbye to the children.

"He's disgusting, and I am not like Mamá."

The bookseller gave her a sympathetic look. Quin slipped his grandfather's envelope carefully into his backpack, where it nestled between the red scarf, the camera, and his sketch pad and colored pencils. He zipped the backpack, then pointed to the painting of the quetzal bird. "Can I buy it?"

Pen shook her head. "That thing? Why?"

He shrugged. "It looks kind of like the Eagle Warrior. And I want to study the difference between the artistry. It might tell us something."

She nodded. "Good thinking." She leaned in and whispered, "See, you have a knack for investigating."

The bookseller took the painting off the wall. "The grandson of El Director may have it for free." He slipped the painting into a manila envelope like the one that held their grandfather's package and handed it to Quin.

He grinned. "Thanks." He turned to Pen. "I think the professor is gone and we should probably get back." She nodded, and they stepped to the door.

"Children," the bookseller called. He frowned and stepped out from behind the counter. "I am not sure I should be telling you this, but that painted book your friend—"

"He's not our friend," she interrupted.

"No, of course not. Well, the book the Spanish man was looking for? It's the same one your grandfather is searching for." He pointed to Quin's backpack. "And what's inside that envelope may be a key. Con cuidado. Take care of it."

Pen gasped. "Do you mean the Codex Cardona?"

The bookseller nodded. "It has been called that, yes, and your grandfather and his friend have asked me through the years to keep an eye out for an ancient manuscript like this. When your grandfather's friend disappeared, I thought Miguel had lost interest, until a few weeks ago."

"What does Abuelito know about the Codex Cardona?" she burst out.

Quin followed with the more troubling question. "Who

disappeared?"

The bookseller shook his head. "That is not my story to tell. You must ask your grandfather. As for the Codex Cardona, it is a mystery to me. If this codex is real, it would be priceless. Not many of our ancestors' painted books survived. Not many of our ancestors survived."

He pointed to the envelope holding the bird painting. "And now, instead of priceless painted books, we make tourist trinkets. Así es la vida." He sounded very much like La Condesa when the children tried to declare something unfair. "That is life."

The bookseller put a finger beneath his eye. "But cuidado, niños. This kind of search sometimes attracts bad people. Your abuelito must be careful, and so should you."

The bookseller retreated to the counter and began wiping the smudge from Professor Flores' elbow with his handkerchief.

The twins left the bookshop and walked in a daze down Madero Street. It was even busier than before as the afternoon slipped away.

"Abuelito knows about the Codex Cardona. He's looking for it," Pen said.

"We have to tell him about the note and Eagle Warrior," Quin said.

"Not yet."

"Didn't you hear what the bookseller said? Abuelito's friend disappeared."

She shrugged. "We don't know what he meant by that. Maybe it means he moved away."

He stopped walking and let others on the street push by him. He gripped the envelope with the quetzal painting in his hand. "You know that's not what he meant. Why would he say disappeared if he meant moved away? When people disappear, it's never for a good reason."

Pen whipped around to face him. "We're just getting started with our investigation. If we look a little more, I bet we can find—" Her eyes widened. "Look out!"

Somebody shoved him from behind. He let go of the envelope in his hands and tried to catch himself, but his hands and knees smacked into the cobblestone street. The rough stones scraped away his skin and jarred him from palms to shoulders. He gritted his teeth and only kept from crying out through the grim determination of a goal keeper.

"Stop," his sister shouted. "Stop him." She raced away. He pushed to his knees in time to see his sister's hair fly as she dodged between people. Ahead of her, someone else was running. Someone holding Quin's manila envelope in his hands.

8

Pen pumped her arms and raced down Madero Street. Ahead of her, Quin's assailant wove between clusters of people, the envelope clutched in his hands. He wore jeans and a red ball cap, but she couldn't see anything more. The assailant reached a crowd waiting to cross the street at a stoplight. She dug deep and sprinted hard. Her lungs burned as she sucked in the city's smog-filled air, but she pushed harder. Pen was almost there. She would catch him.

The tackle came from behind. Her momentum drove her hard into the pavement. Air whooshed out of her lungs. Her hands and elbows scraped rough stone and made her cry out. She rolled over and checked her elbows. Blood seeped from raw scratches. A red splotch stained the newly ripped knee of her jeans. Her entire body felt like a peeled mango. She pulled her phone from her pocket. Luckily, it wasn't broken.

Around her, people stared, open-mouthed. Pen struggled to her feet, unsteady and oxygen-deprived, and whirled to face her attacker. Quin lay sprawled on the ground, reaching for his glasses that must have fallen off when he tackled her.

"You—" Disbelief coursed through her. "But I had him," she cried out. And just as her brother stood up, she shoved him in the chest. Hard.

He fell backwards and landed on his butt. His glasses went flying again. At the shock on his face, she instantly regretted her actions, but anger still boiled inside her. "I was going to get it back," she said furiously. "I could almost see his face."

Quin's mouth opened and closed a couple of times and he blinked hard. His face went pomegranate red. He leaped up. "Get what back? A cheap souvenir? From a thief?"

He grabbed her hand and jerked her down the street. "We have to get out of here. When that thief finds out he has the quetzal bird and not a real painting, he'll be angry."

His reasoning oozed through Pen's anger like the blood on her knee. The thief had taken the envelope in her brother's hands, not his backpack. He stole the cheap painting. Quin was right. That made her even madder. But they didn't have time to argue. They needed to leave the scene.

"There." Pen pointed as a bus pulled up to a stop across the street. They hurried to it and climbed on.

"Where's it going?" her twin asked as they shuffled to the back and found a seat.

"Doesn't matter." She sat and Quin plopped down beside her. The bus roared away and turned off Madero Street, taking them away from their assailant.

"I can't believe you tackled me." Her knees and hands stung badly enough to bring tears to her eyes. Next to her, Quin examined his own injuries.

"I had to. What were you going to do when you caught the thief? Ask him nicely to give back the painting he stole? For once, could you think ahead even a little?"

Pen stared out the window and swallowed hard, stung by her brother's words. He was right. She hadn't thought what she would do when she caught up to the thief. What kind of investigator was she turning out to be? Her hands shook, and not from the scrapes on her palms.

"Thanks," she finally whispered, not looking at him.

"You're welcome," he muttered back. They stared out the window in silence as the bus rolled through parts of Mexico City completely unfamiliar to them.

"I only caught up to you because I grew two inches this year."

Pen stared down at her hands, knowing he was offering to make up. She had no reason to be angry with him, so she tried to force her sullenness away and nodded. "Maybe you should play forward instead of me."

"Nah, I don't want to be that close to Michael Blalock."

"That's— he's not—" she sputtered. Her face grew hot.

Quin shook his head and fought a smile. "I think we should get off this bus and figure out how to get back to the house before Abuela has la policia out looking for us."

Three buses later, the twins climbed down at the end of their grandparents' street. The jacaranda trees she'd always loved lined the road with their deep green foliage and low-hanging branches. They'd taken the wrong bus once, but an old woman had helped them catch the right one back to their grandparents' neighborhood, but not before they were late for dinner. The twins hurried past the houses. Pen hoped Abuela wouldn't be too mad at them. Her mind turned back to Quin's attacker.

"Who do you think it was?" she whispered, even though there was no reason to.

Her brother shook his head. "Who even knew we were at the bookshop? What did the thief look like?"

"I don't know. It happened so fast and there were people everywhere." She frowned and tried to think back. If only he had tackled her a second later. "What about Professor Flores?"

"What about him?"

"I don't trust him. Remember the way he looked at that envelope? Maybe he took it." She tried to remember if she'd seen a greasy ponytail slip from the red cap of Quin's assailant.

"Why would he steal it?" Quin asked. "But you're right. I don't trust him either."

Their grandparents' home sat on the end of the street, a once grand white stucco house with red roof tiles and white columns on either side of the front porch, a remnant from colonial Mexico. Pen grabbed his arm as he started up the steps.

He turned, a frown flitting across his face. "What is it? We're late."

"Shouldn't we look at whatever's in that envelope? I mean, that's what the thief wanted. He doesn't know he stole the quetzal bird instead."

"He does now." He hesitated, then shook his head. "It feels wrong, and whatever it is, we know someone wants to steal it. I think we should tell Abuelito."

Her face fell. "That means we'll have to tell him about the website and being international investigators. Then it's back to a boring summer cleaning house for La Condesa."

Quin tried to straighten his glasses, but they still sat askew on his nose. "I guess we don't have to tell him about the website yet. Just the envelope."

She nodded, looking relieved. "Good. Let's get inside. I want to contact our client tonight and update him."

"Niños?" Abuela called as soon as they walked in. It was shadowy in the hallway, but light flowed through the kitchen door at the end of the hall. Their grandmother stood silhouetted in the doorway, the light shining through her white hair pulled elegantly into a loose bun.

She advanced upon them brandishing a wooden spoon like a general with his sword. "Where have you been? What were you thinking?" She peppered the twins with questions and didn't wait for an answer.

Abuelito saved them. He came through the open courtyard and greeted them with a quiet "Buenas tardes," then asked the twins a question.

"Did you get my package, mis hijos?"

The twins exchanged a surprised look. Quin nodded.

"What package?" Abuela asked.

"An errand I sent them on this afternoon. Can you give us a few minutes before dinner, mi amor?"

Their grandmother sighed and lifted her nose. "The pozole and tortillas are hot now. I will fill your bowls." She spun and whisked away with a swirl of her skirt. Abuelito laughed softly.

"How did you know about the package?" Quin asked.

Their grandfather pushed them through the portico into the atrium. "My friend from the bookshop called. He had second thoughts about giving my package to children." He sighed. "I've been worried about you for hours. I was thinking of searching for you myself—without telling your grandmother, of course."

"We took the wrong bus." Her brother shot her a dubious look. It wasn't exactly a lie.

They crossed the courtyard, past Abuela's banana and orange trees, into Abuelito's office. The home office was the one place Abuela was forbidden to clean thoroughly, and even then, the bookshelves on two walls showed signs of a recent dusting. Books overflowed into stacks on the floor, some with pristine covers and others so worn they might have been as old as the codex itself. Quin could see why his grandfather was the shop owner's favorite customer.

The old man sat in a large leather chair and gestured for the children to sit on a matching loveseat half covered in books. They placed the books gingerly on the floor and complied.

"Now." Abuelito rubbed his hands together. "Let's see what you've brought me."

Quin took the envelope from his backpack and his grandfather reached for it, but he drew back.

Abuelito furrowed his eyebrows. "What is it, m'ijo?" he asked, his gentle words nearly bringing tears to Quin's eyes."

"Tell him," Pen said.

He told his grandfather about running into Professor Flores in the bookstore, getting the quetzal bird painting, and walking out with the envelope in his hands. Then his sister jumped in with how someone knocked Quin to the ground and stole the envelope. She left out the part about chasing the assailant. Her brother bit his lip but didn't tell, either.

"Whoever it was must have thought Quin was holding your envelope. What's inside it?"

The old man sat as still as one of the stone heads. His face was even more terrible, dark and flushed. "Dios mio. If I thought you children were in danger, I would have come as soon as the bookseller called me. I should have known something like this could—"

He sprang to life suddenly, placing a hand on each twin's cheek. "Estan bien?" he asked them. "You're not hurt?"

He frowned at the bloodstains on their knees and the scrapes on their hands and elbows. "I've had worse after a soccer game," Quin reassured him.

Pen nodded. "Me too. Estamos bien, Abuelito," she added in Spanish, just to reassure him. He put a hand on her cheek and gripped her brother's shoulder. "Gracias a Dios," he murmured. He released them and sat down. "I could never forgive myself if you were hurt, not to mention what your grandmother would do to me."

"Death by chile pepper?" he suggested.

Their grandfather chuckled, but she wouldn't be put off by her brother's joke. "But what's in the envelope? Why would somebody try to steal it?"

"Ah." Abuelito grew grave and took the envelope out of Quin's hands. He placed it on his desk and tapped it with one finger. "I received an email earlier in the week to expect a delivery. No signature. The address was unfamiliar to me and when I replied, it came back as undeliverable."

"So you do turn on your computer."

The old man laughed at her words. "I'm not as far behind the times as you think, Penelope. I just prefer old-
fashioned letters. You have to think longer about what you
want to say, and once you send those words, you can't take
them back."

Abuelito studied the envelope in his hands. "As for
what's inside and who sent it, I'm not sure, but I have a
theory." He opened the clasp and slid out a brown sheet of
paper, thicker than normal, and held it out for the twins to
see. An Aztec woman in a white dress placed tortillas on a
flat baking stone.

"She's beautiful," she whispered. She couldn't take her
eyes off the woman's warm gaze. Her black eyes seemed to
peer straight into Pen's soul.

The paper rippled, and the woman's smile flashed at
her as if to say hello. Pen stepped back and shook her head.
Her brother's constant lectures over artwork must be getting to her. She could have sworn the tortilla maker
winked.

"Dios mio."

Her grandfather's whispered exclamation sent an unexpected shiver down her back. "What is it?"

"This is a piece of a puzzle I've been trying to solve for
forty years," the old man said quietly. "One I'd given up
on."

His voice held such grief, Pen looked up, alarmed. He
set the painting on his desk and continued to stare at the
tortilla maker. "If I'm correct, niños, this is a page from a
painted book called the Codex Cardona."

9

Pen felt as if a bolt of lightning had struck her. She practically buzzed with electricity. When she finally found her voice, it came out high-pitched.

"But you said the only painted book in Mexico was in your museum. Where did this page come from? How old is it? Why didn't you tell us about the Codex Cardona?"

Abuelito held up his hand to stem her questions. His eyes grew distant, like he was looking across time only he could see.

"Could it be?" he whispered. "After all this time and no word?" He reached out and caressed the painting as gently as he'd touched Pen's cheek. "Francisco?"

The twins looked at each other and shrugged.

"Who's Francisco?" they asked at the same time. She reached out to pinch her brother, but he batted her hand away and threw her an irritated look. Right. Now was not the time for a jinx.

Abuelito cleared his throat and rubbed his eyes beneath his spectacles. "Un amigo. I lost track of him several years ago."

She didn't know what to make of his words. Did he mean they used to be friends and then had a fight like she and Eileen Esposito, who'd asked Michael Blalock to the spring dance knowing how much Pen liked him? Or did her grandfather mean his friend was really lost?

Quin was making weird faces at her and mouthing something. "The bookshop owner. Lost friend." She had gotten good at lip-reading. Her brother constantly mouthed things to her across the classroom at school.

Abuelito pulled a magnifying glass out of his desk, snapped on a bright lamp, and began examining the painting closely. Quin stood and leaned over their grandfather's shoulder. Clearly, he understood what the old man was doing. Pen stared at the painting, trying to see what they did. Powerful strokes, granules of paint stuck in the lines, and above all, those brilliant colors—colors so bright they filled you with hope that somewhere in the world, life like this still existed.

She stared into the tortilla maker's dark eyes and felt time falling away between them. *Camila,* she thought. *That's her name.* And her tortillas were the best in the village, with just the right amount of corn, never sticking to the clay oven. Her smile confirmed the theory. She was proud of Pen for knowing. For understanding.

"Is it real?" Quin whispered.

She blinked and shook her head. *Stop being silly,* she told herself. *Paintings don't talk.* Camila's eyes twinkled at her anyway.

Abuelito set down the magnifying glass and leaned back, releasing a low whistle. "If it isn't, Quintus, it is the best fake I've ever seen."

Quin reached out slowly and touched the painting, just on the corner where no paint coated it. "How old is it?"

"If it's the real Codex Cardona, over four hundred and fifty years old."

He yanked his hand back as if burned by a hot tortilla. Mamá and Kostas always told them not to touch old artifacts with bare hands. Something to do with oily fingers. Professor Flores must have ruined many artifacts with his fingers, Pen thought.

"What do you mean, if it's real?" she asked.

"Bueno," Abuelito hesitated. "Let me explain. I first heard of this book many years ago, when I was in graduate school. My friend Francisco and I tried to track it down, but our search came to nothing. Through the years, it has appeared, but for a few hours or days. Usually for sale by a mystery seller. A museum or university would contact us, and we would hurry to see it, but it was always too late. By the time we arrived, the book and its seller had vanished. Francisco became so obsessed with the search, he let everything else go. His wife, his work at the museum in Spain, and even—" Here, Abeulito's voice thickened. "Even old friendships. And one day, he simply disappeared, along with any mention of the Codex Cardona."

"Wow," Quin whispered.

"But where's the rest of it? This is only one page." Pen reached out and touched the page. It felt real to her, not like it would disappear.

Abuelito rubbed his forehead. "I don't know, m'ija. Not many people know of the Cardona, but those who do will do anything to get their hands on it. And this particular book is said to be cursed."

The words sent shivers racing down her spine. Her brother raised his eyebrows at her, asking a silent question. *Shouldn't we tell him about our search?*

She frowned and shook her head, turning back to their grandfather before he could notice the twins' unspoken communication. "Cursed how?"

"People who get close to it are sometimes never seen again. Francisco and I used to laugh at that before he disappeared."

They stared at the painting as if the tortilla maker had the power to tell them where she'd come from and if the curse was real.

"If this painting is really part of the Codex Cardona," Quin said slowly, "then someone has found it. Someone knows where the painted book is."

"And they want to make sure you know too, Abuelito,"

Pen cried.

"That is what concerns me." The old man pointed to the unmarked envelope. "No return address. No note. Why has this painting shown up on my desk now?" He jumped and grabbed his chest as if having a heart attack.

"Abuelito," both children cried.

He gasped, then laughed as he drew a buzzing phone out of his shirt pocket. "Ay, this thing. I nearly die from fright every time somebody calls me."

Pen leaned back on the loveseat cushions and put a hand over her own pounding heart. If something were to happen to him...

"Hello?" He held the phone away from his ear as La Condesa's voice blasted through. "Si, mi amor. At once."

Abuelito ended the call, his face so grave Pen wondered if the world was ending. "Children," he announced. "Dinner is now cold."

He slid the painting into its envelope, placed it in the top desk drawer, and turned a small key to lock it. The key went into his pocket with his phone.

"But the codex," Pen protested.

Her grandfather patted her shoulder. "We'll talk more later. We cannot keep La Condesa waiting. And if I were you"—he ushered the children back into the courtyard—"I would take care with the peppers in the stew."

The spicy stew turned in Pen's stomach long after she'd gone to bed. Quin tossed and turned in the bed next to hers, muttering indistinguishable sounds. She couldn't get used to hearing someone else's breathing and wished for the quiet of her own bedroom at home, broken only by the soft buzz of the fan on her laptop.

"Anna?" he mumbled. Her ears perked up. Was that Anna Callahan, her best friend? She sat up and whispered, "What about Anna?" but her brother was asleep. She tucked that question away for later and decided to get up.

Pen picked up her phone and laptop and carried them both to the window seat. Cool night air flowed into the room. Muted music and laughter drifted out through the patio doors of a café across the street. She opened Odyssey and clicked on the alpha symbol. Archie's location popped up, and she smiled and typed:

π: Out on a date?

While she waited for a reply, she flipped open her laptop and pulled up the website. She felt a thrill rush through her as she read the words she'd written again: *International Agents of Intrigue.* She couldn't believe she was involved with an actual ancient mystery, just like Mamá. Even better. The phone dinged, and Pen scanned Archie's response.

α: Wouldn't you like to know? Why up so late?

π: Spicy food. Can't sleep.

α: Sounds like La Condesa! Trouble?

Pen paused. How did Archie always know? It was like he had an older brother superpower. She thought about the day, from retrieving the red scarf and the Eagle Warrior painting to Quin being knocked down outside the bookshop. Then there was the Codex Cardona and Abuelito's lost friend. Her head spun with it all. She could barely hold it in. Her finger hovered over her keypad. If she told him about the website, he would keep her secret. But would he stay silent over the painted book? He was as fun and as smart as could be, but he was still her older brother. She sighed and typed:

π: No problemas, mi hermano.

α: Buenas noches, hermanita. Go to bed.

She closed the app, feeling guilty. Pen hadn't lied to Archie. She didn't have a problem; she had a mystery to solve, and she wanted to do it by herself. Her twin snorted in his sleep. Well, maybe with Quin's help, she thought. She turned to the laptop and went through her security protocols. The website inbox popped up with one new message.

Pen swallowed, glanced at her brother, and opened the message.

An unexpected complication came up this morning. I trust you got my message. We need to meet face to face.

Pen thought about the red scarf from the zoo, the man in the red hat who stole Quin's quetzal bird painting and finally, Camila. Where did it all lead? Did they actually have a page of the Codex Cardona? Was the book truly cursed? She nodded to herself and hit reply.

Café Azteca across from the Museo Nacional. When can we meet?

She clicked send. Goosebumps popped up on her arms. The night chill, she told herself. She checked her regular mail and skimmed a letter from Anna. Michael sent her a short one that read,

No good forwards at camp. Too bad you're not here, Penhead.

Archie's nickname for her made her smile. Pen realized she didn't regret not being at soccer camp anymore. Finding the Codex Cardona was more important. She snapped the laptop shut.

"Anna?" Quin mumbled from the bed.

She would definitely have to ask her brother tomorrow why he was dreaming about her best friend. She slipped into bed, the peppers finally settling in her stomach, and dreamed of making corn tortillas under Camila's skillful direction with the warm sun on her back.

10

The next morning, Quin awoke eager to find out more about the codex, but Abuela had other ideas.

"La fiesta es mañana. We have much to do." After a breakfast of fresh fruit and huevos rancheros, she set the twins to dusting the salon where the fiesta would be held. When she disappeared down the hall, Pen filled him in on the note from their client to meet face to face.

"You decided that without me?" He rubbed at invisible dust on one of the bookshelves.

"Well, I would have decided with you, but you were sleeping," she tossed back. "And dreaming about Anna."

"I was not." He turned away from his twin so she couldn't see his face. "And sleeping is what normal people do at night."

"It's overrated." She yawned so loudly Abuela laughed when she entered the room. "So you're already ready for your siesta?" She set down a tray with two bottles of bubbly mineral water. "I brought refrescos. You're doing such a good job. Next, let's shake out the rugs and sweep the floor."

She turned to leave, and Pen mimed hitting her head on the bookcase. Quin smiled at her antics. He gave his sister a conciliatory eye roll at La Condesa's back, but secretly, he felt relieved. After the robbery, he wasn't sure he wanted the investigation to continue. He couldn't help but wonder how angry the thief was when he discovered he'd stolen the quetzal bird, not a four-hundred-and-fifty-year-old tortilla maker. How had the thief even known they had a page from the codex? And then there was the whole curse thing Abuelito mentioned. Just thinking about that made his stomach feel queasy. Or maybe it was the extra helping from breakfast.

After sweeping the entire salon and entry hall, the twins hung signs that read, *Keep history in the present,* and *Preserving the past for the future.*

"Why does Abuelito need to raise money?" Quin asked. "Isn't it the museo nacional? Doesn't the government give money to it?"

Abuela nodded. "Sí, but this is one way for Miguel to bring private collectors together and encourage them to support the museum, too."

It sounded strange to him to hear anyone call his grandfather by his given name. Abuelito was simply Abuelito.

"Is that why Professor Flores is here?" Pen mimicked the way the professor smoothed his hair and eyebrows while La Condesa's back was turned. Quin smothered a laugh.

"Yes. José Luis has become an important patron of your grandfather's work. In the last year, he has worked closely with Miguel to secure Mexican art originally taken from Mexico to Spain. In fact, he has a private collection himself. Maria said you saw it when you visited him in Spain."

"More like he showed it off," his sister muttered.

"Don't mumble," La Condesa called. She re-dusted a bookshelf Pen had already cleaned. "If you have something to say, say it, m'ija."

"Mamá never has anything good to say about private collectors. She says they buy ancient artifacts on the black market just to hide them away in their homes instead of placing them where the world can enjoy them. She says buying art on the black market makes them thieves as well." Pen frowned at the thought of her mother. What was she doing while the twins followed La Condesa's every command? She tied a ribbon around the end of a sign and stretched it across a bookcase.

Quin thought about the Eagle Warrior hidden inside his backpack. Did that make him an art thief? Shouldn't the warrior be on display for people to see his courage and focus?

"That's just what your grandfather would say about private collectors," Abuela agreed. "He and your mother are like two drops of water." She sighed. "But collectors often know more about the art market than museum directors. Your grandfather calls this 'research.'" She looked around the salon. "Bueno. This will suffice, and your grandfather is bringing tamales for lunch. Quin, please set the table. Pen, help me with la ensalada."

Somehow, La Condesa was always right. Abuelito arrived at that moment and the twins enjoyed lunch on the patio, even with mineral water instead of sodas. At the end of the meal, Abuela announced they would go shopping later for appropriate clothes for the party, but the twins could now go to their room to rest. She didn't leave other options available.

Their grandfather laughed at the looks on their faces when La Condesa disappeared into the kitchen. He got up from the table and retrieved his briefcase. "I brought you something to look over during your siesta. Unless, of course, you truly want to nap."

"Don't tease," Pen protested. "What did you bring us?"

Abuelito pulled a brown file folder from his bag. "These are some notes I took years ago on the Codex Cardona. I thought you might like to look at them."

"Wow," Quin breathed, opening the folder and rummaging through a stack of notebook paper filled with his grandfather's tiny scrawl. "This is a lot of information."

"I thought you weren't looking for the Codex Cardona anymore," his sister said. "Did you change your mind?"

He glanced toward the kitchen and lowered his voice. "After Francisco disappeared, I promised your grandmother I would stop searching for the book. She thinks it's too dangerous." He sighed, and his wrinkles deepened. "But I haven't stopped searching for Francisco."

"We can help you," Pen said.

"No," Abuelito said so sharply Quin looked up from the notes. "Gracias, mis hijos, but no. Even with the arrival of this painting, I think we should leave the Codex Cardona in the past."

He returned to the museum and the twins retired to their room, shut the door, and spread the contents of the file across Quin's neatly made bed.

"This is amazing." He scanned the dates at the top of the notes. "It says the Cardona contains over four hundred pages of paintings and details of Aztec life."

Pen read through one of the notes. "This says someone, probably a private collector," she said with the same disdain Mamá would have, "tried to sell the codex at several American and British auctions and universities, but nobody would buy it because they couldn't decide if it was authentic or not."

"Why?" He leafed through some old copies of paintings that looked similar to the sketch of the Eagle Warrior from Abuelito's desk. Each sketch had a tiny FR in the corner of the page.

"Hmm. Lots of reasons." She continued to read. "The codex is painted on Aztec paper instead of Spanish royal paper, and nobody could say where it came from, who wrote it, and where it's been for the last four hundred years." She stopped reading. "It appeared out of nowhere."

"But that happens. Mamá's found rare artifacts nobody knew existed." Quin pulled the Eagle Warrior carefully from his backpack and, laying the red scarf aside, smoothed the painting's corners until it lay open next to the notes. The corners still curled inward, so he laid the heavy art book from his parents on the top and held the bottom corners with his thumbs.

The dark brown paper contrasted sharply with their grandfather's notes. He started to trace the spear with his finger, then remembered he shouldn't touch the ink.

"Why would our client send us this?" he asked. "How did he get it? And who sent the tortilla maker to Abuelito? Do you think it was the same person? Or someone else?"

"I don't know." Pen hardly ever admitted to not knowing something. Her response troubled him. "But Abuelito's not the only one looking for this painted book."

"Maybe that's why he is scared. Did you see his face at lunch? That's why he asked us not to help him."

Pen stiffened and set down the notes. "Our client doesn't know we're his grandchildren. I bet he doesn't even know about Abuelito. And maybe he has a good reason to find the Codex Cardona, just like Abuelito does. That's why he hired us."

Quin pursed his lips. He wasn't so sure, but he had another question lurking in the back of his mind. "Pen, what if the curse is real?"

His sister shook her head. "That's silly superstition." S sounded more like Mamá than ever. She went back to reading the notes. He looked at the Eagle Warrior on the bed. The warrior's lips were pressed firmly together. What secrets was he hiding?

"Listen to this." She read from the notes. "A Spanish monk named Bernardino de Sahagún lived with the Aztecs for sixty years. He was responsible for another painted book somewhere in…" She flipped through the notes. "I can't find the next page."

"Here's his name again." Quin pointed to Abuelito's scribbles. "And again on this page." Pen joined in, searching through the notes and looking for the slanted capital B denoting the name Bernardino. They found more references to the famous monk.

"He talks about Bernardino almost as if he's alive, not a monk who lived four hundred years ago. And what does an old Spanish monk have to do with our painted book?"

"I don't know." She sighed. "But that's what international agents of intrigue do, they investigate."

Quin dumped the folder of Abuelito's notes onto the bed and slipped the Eagle Warrior into the folder to protect it. He probably shouldn't be carrying a four-hundred-year-old painting rolled up in his backpack. A breeze swept through the window and sent chills down his arms. He couldn't believe it. They were uncovering something mysterious. Something important. Just like Pen said they would.

"So what's next?" He almost dreaded the answer.

His sister grabbed her laptop and pulled up the website. Her face fell. "No new emails. She sighed and closed the laptop. "I guess, for now, we wait."

He started collecting the papers and putting them back in the file, examining each one as he did so.

Abuela rapped sharply at the door. "Are you awake, children? It's time to go shopping. You have five minutes to meet me at the front door." Her heels clicked as she walked away.

Pen groaned. "An international mystery to solve and we have to go shopping for party clothes with La Condesa. You know she'll make me get a dress."

Quin grinned. "Probably." He put the file folder holding the Eagle Warrior and Abuelito's notes into his backpack.

"You're taking it with you?" she asked. "Even after what happened yesterday?"

He nodded. "We'll be with La Condesa. Nobody would dare rob her."

Shopping with La Condesa was not for the faint hearted. She perused, tested, pinched, and tucked, ordered, rejected, clucked her tongue, and finally, approved. "You look as sharp as Abuelito," she told Quin, nodding at the white button-down shirt and dark slacks she'd chosen for him.

"I look like a waiter," he muttered when his grand-mother disappeared to find yet another dress for Pen to try on. She scowled at her twin. "At least you're wearing pants, not a dress."

She tried in vain to steer Abuela to more modern dresses. If she had to wear one, at least she could be fash-ionable. Her grandmother dismissed each of her sugges-tions as too short, too thin, and too showy. After an interminable parade of dresses, Abuela clicked her tongue.

"Wait here," she advised her granddaughter, leaving her staring forlornly into a changing room mirror. She re-turned with a flowing white dress embroidered in red. The skirt was long and fluffy, and the neckline plunged like Ni-agara Falls. Pen stared, dismayed.

"But, Abuela," she protested, "I'll look like a flamenco dancer."

La Condesa lifted her slight shoulders. "What is wrong with that? Flamenco is a fine Spanish dance."

She gritted her teeth and took the dress. When she emerged from the dressing room for the fifteenth time, Abuela gasped and clapped. Even Quin's eyebrows shot up. She turned to the mirror and examined her reflection. The dress was long, but she did like the way it showed off her shoulders. She wondered what Michael Blalock would say.

"You look just like Maria," her grandmother said.

Pen frowned into the mirror. She'd kept Mamá from her mind with the excitement over the painted book. Abuela pressed her lips together. "It's a shame your mother insists on dressing like a man on those field trips of hers."

"They're digs to ancient ruins," she protested. "She can't wear a dress to them."

The old lady grunted and motioned for both the twins to go change. "Well, she can at least see pictures of how preciosos her daughter and son are."

Abuela asked them to pass their clothing over the

dressing room doors and when the twins came out in their jeans and t-shirts, the clothes were already wrapped up and paid for. Their grandmother handed them each a bag. "And now for jewelry and a tie."

Quin's eyes bugged out and she smirked at him. "Serves you right."

"Abuela," he said, but a haunting melody of a Spanish waltz interrupted him.

"Abuela, you have a phone, too?" Pen asked.

La Condesa pulled the phone from her purse and silenced the waltz. "To keep track of your grandfather." She barely contained her smile, then put the phone to her ear.

"She'll probably start texting us next," Quin whispered. "Don't let her find out about Odyssey. She'll want to keep tabs on everyone."

She covered her mouth in mock horror at the idea of La Condesa keeping track of them twenty-four hours a day. "So much for being international agents then." Pen turned to her to make sure she hadn't overheard their joke and froze. Abuela's eyes had clouded over and she gripped the phone with both hands.

"Qué pasó?" Pen cried. She'd never seen Abuela look so pale.

"Ahora vamos," Her grandmother spoke into the phone. She ended the call and slipped the phone into her purse. Her eyes were on the children but looking through them at something they couldn't see.

"Abuela, what's wrong?" Pen shook her arm in a way she'd never dare in normal circumstances.

Her action brought the old lady out of her daze. She grasped her arm and reached for Quin's shoulder. Her fingers dug in, and Pen felt her fear in the tight grip.

"Your grandfather. He's been attacked."

11

Abuela gave little details on the taxi ride to the hospital. Abuelito's secretary found him unconscious in his office, and it appeared someone had hit him over the head. Quin polished his glasses furiously and tried not to think why his grandfather had been attacked.

When they arrived, a nurse informed them Abuelito was in an intensive care room and no one under sixteen was allowed inside. She frowned at the twins when she said this. Abuela hustled them to the elevator and they stepped off on the third floor. She waved the two of them to a set of hard chairs in the hall and disappeared inside the room. The door clicked behind her and the twins slumped into the chairs, still gripping their shopping bags. Quin stared at the bag. Who cared about fiestas when Abuelito was hurt?

"Do you think he's okay?" Pen whispered.

He glanced at his sister. She didn't often look defense-less, but her face was pale, and her dark eyes brimmed with tears. She swallowed several times.

He stared at his sneakers. He hated it when she started to cry. It rarely happened. His shoes were covered in street dust and scuffed from his fall yesterday. "I don't know. I hate waiting."

She nodded. The elevator dinged and a man wearing a

dark blue police uniform approached them. He nodded their way and started toward the door.

"Perdón," Quin called out, surprising himself and Pen. He jumped up. "That's our grandfather. Can you tell us what happened? Is he okay?"

The policeman studied them, his eyes serious. "I don't know. That's why I'm here myself." He started to enter the room but paused. "You don't know why someone would hurt your grandfather, do you? It appears the assailant was searching for something in his office."

Pen sucked in her breath and he knew they shared the same thought. They knew of only one reason someone would attack Abuelito. The Codex Cardona.

Quin lost his boldness. He stared at the policeman's shiny black boots and rubbed his palms on his jeans.

"We only came to visit our grandparents a few days ago," his sister said.

The officer nodded curtly. "Of course. If you think of anything, make sure you tell us." He entered Abuelito's room and the twins sank into their chairs again.

"Should we have told him what we know?" Quin asked.

Pen shrugged. "Told him what? We don't know much, and everything about the search for the Codex Cardona sounds crazy, anyway." She put her head in her hands. Her hair draped across her face, masking it from him, but he didn't need to see her face to know how she felt.

"Do you think it's the curse?"

She lifted her head slightly and peeked out at him through strands of hair. "Curses don't exist.".

Quin drew his knees up to his chest and tucked his chin on top. Two days ago, he would have agreed with his sister. Now, he wasn't so sure.

When Abuela finally emerged, she had shrunk from La Condesa to an old woman. Her skin was too pale and the veins on the hands she held out to them too blue. The twins jumped up and hugged her.

"Your grandfather has a serious concussion," Abuela said. Quin was suddenly glad for his grandmother's tendency to speak frankly. "He hasn't awoken since he got here." She caught her breath and put one hand on her heart. "The doctor isn't sure when that might happen."

He felt his grandmother's words sink in. *If*, he thought. *She means* if *Abuelito will wake up.*

"What does that mean?" Pen asked. "Is Abuelito…"

"It means I must stay with him," Abuela said firmly. "I've spoken with your mother. I want you to take a taxi straight to the house and wait. Your mother will call soon, and we will decide what to do if—" She paused and cleared her throat. "We will make a decision."

The twins climbed into one of several taxis waiting outside the hospital. They both stared silently out the window at the shops and restaurants full of people enjoying the cooler evening air. How dare they? Didn't they know the world had changed? Quin thought.

He thought about the police officer's question and the answer they hadn't given. What would the police think if he told them about the Codex Cardona? Maybe it wasn't the curse, but somebody attacked Abuelito the day after he received a page from the codex. It couldn't be a coincidence. He didn't like his next thought, but he couldn't keep it from popping out of his mouth.

"We have to go to Abuelito's office."

Pen half grinned. "I like the way you're thinking, but the museum's closed. We'll have to go in the morning."

He nodded. He was usually the levelheaded twin. He should have thought of that.

"Besides," she whispered. "I think we have what the attacker was looking for." She patted Quin's backpack lying on the seat between them, and he remembered the folder of notes and the Aztec Warrior painting he'd stuffed inside before they went shopping.

"Do you think since Abuelito's notes on the codex

weren't in his office, we'll be safe at the house?"

Quin inhaled sharply. "I hadn't thought of that."

"Neither did Abuela."

He gripped the backpack. "I guess we'll find out."

The taxi pulled up in front of the house and they paid the driver and hopped out. The twins stood outside, studying the house. Birds chirped to each other from leafy perches in the jacarandas. Music drifted from the café across the street. Everything seemed peaceful. They opened the front door with the key Abuela gave them. The entry hall was dark. Quin stumbled along the wall and turned the light on quickly, revealing an empty hallway.

"Let's go together." Pen grasped his hand, something she hadn't done in years. They hurried down the hall into the kitchen, flipping light switches. Once there, they turned around and dashed across the atrium to the bedrooms. When those were lit, only Abuelito's office remained. He had started to relax. They'd turned on nearly every light in the house with no sign of an intruder. Still, his imagination played tricks on him as they crossed the atrium again. He imagined crouching figures behind the giant leaves of the banana tree.

His sister paused outside the closed office door. "One...two...three," she counted, the way they used to when they were little and wanted to spring inside and frighten Abuelito.

"Yaaaaah," he shouted as he thrust open the door.

Pen dashed to the wall and hit the light switch. The light nearly blinded them after the darkness of the atrium. He squinted. They were the only two in the room.

She collapsed onto the loveseat. "Yaaah? Was that going to scare away an intruder?"

Quin shrugged and gave her a weak grin. He sat in Abuelito's chair, but it felt so unnatural he immediately stood up. "Let's go back—" He looked down and stared at the desk.

"What is it?" Pen asked.

"Didn't Abuelito lock this drawer and put the key in his pocket?"

Pen stood and walked over to him. "Yes. He put it inside his shirt pocket with his phone. Remember, the phone vibrated in his pocket and scared him, and we thought he was having a heart attack—

She stopped talking.

"Right." Quin pretended not to see the tears budding at the corner of her eyes. "It's not locked now."

They both stared silently at the desk drawer, now slightly ajar.

"Maybe Abuelito came back while we were shopping," Pen whispered.

He slid the drawer open slowly. It was empty. The painting from the Codex Cardona was gone.

12

Neither twin wanted to light Abuela's finicky gas stove, so they ate cold tortillas and leftovers in the kitchen. Pen's phone rang, and she swallowed a mouthful of food with a grimace. How could tortillas taste so amazing when hot and so awful when cold?

"Hello," she mumbled through a mouthful of dry tortilla.

"Penelope, estás bien?" Maria Grey-Reyes asked on the other end. Pen hated to cry, but her mother's voice made her blink rapidly.

"Si, Mamá. We both are." Quin pushed his plate aside. She set the phone on the table and hit speaker.

Hearing the distress in their mother's voice was difficult, but the twins had decided not to say anything about the codex yet. The stolen painting was the only thing missing from the house, as far as they could tell. There were no signs of a break-in, either. In fact, without talking to Abuelito, they couldn't be sure the painting had been stolen. Perhaps their grandfather had just taken it back to the museum or somewhere else. But he couldn't tell them right now.

"I can't get a flight from here until later in the week." Mamá was currently on one of the tiny Greek islands with a group of archeology students and professors. "I can take the ferry, but it will take me nearly as long as waiting for a plane, and I'm scheduled to give a lecture in the morning. I'm going to talk to Abuela first thing mañana and see if Abuelito is better before I decide."

Pen felt anger flare within her. Their grandfather was lying unconscious and Mamá was questioning whether she should be bothered with changing her travel plans?

Quin frowned at her and shook his head slightly. "We understand. Abuelito could wake up any moment. He wouldn't want you to miss your lectures."

"Or he could never wake up," she mumbled. He shot her an anguished look and she immediately regretted her words. Neither of them had voiced this concern, but it had lurked in their minds all afternoon like shadows in the atrium, dark and menacing.

"What was that, m'ija?" Mamá asked. "The connection cut out."

"Nothing."

They talked a little of the attack, but the twins had few details and Mamá had talked to the police herself. After a few minutes, she assured them Abuela would return home soon and they would talk again in the morning.

After they hung up, the twins scraped the remaining food from their plates, washed them, and went to their room. Without their grandparents at home, every little noise made them jump. A scratching on the windowpane turned out to be the thorns of one of their grandmother's coveted yellow rose bushes growing in the atrium. Quin closed their bedroom door and actually turned the lock, but Pen reminded him Abuela would want to check on them when she got home. For once, she was glad they shared this room.

She took off her shoes and threw them on the floor. "Who would want to hurt Abuelito?" she cried out.

Quin crisscrossed his legs and tucked his chin in his hands. "When Abuelito told us about the codex last night, did you think there were things he wasn't telling us?"

She rolled her eyes. "There are always things they're not telling us." Maybe that's why she wanted to be an investigator. She was tired of being left out.

Pen wound her hair around her index finger, something she did when she was perplexed. She stopped and pulled out the tangles. "Someone else is looking for the codex, and they found out Abuelito had a page. That's why he was attacked. And that's why the painting from the desk is gone." She swallowed and glanced at the closed door. Just knowing someone else had been inside the house made her feel unsafe.

Quin nodded. "It's the only thing that makes sense. And it explains why Abuelito asked us not to help him find the codex and why he gave up on finding his friend, too."

She held still. "You mean, Abuelito knew of the danger?"

He shrugged. "Maybe. Either way, we're the only ones who know why he was attacked. And the only ones who still have a page from the codex."

"One person knows about it," Pen corrected. "Our client." She retrieved her laptop and pulled up the website inbox. "He replied," she told him, her heart thumping. He leaped off his bed and plopped down beside her. They read the message together.

Tomorrow. Café Azteca. 11 a.m. Come alone. We are in danger.

She read the email three times before speaking. "Danger," she whispered. Next to her, Quin shuddered. She felt fear swell inside her. This was her fault. She'd created the website. She convinced her brother to go along with her and not tell anyone else. It was supposed to be fun. Now, Abuelito was in the hospital and they were in danger. Unnamed, unknown danger.

Both twins jumped when the door opened. They hadn't heard Abuela come home.

"Lo siento," she apologized, seeing their startled faces. She gave them a tired smile. "This house can be curiosa at night. I've often felt restless the nights your grandfather is away." Her smile faded as they all remembered tonight was one of those nights.

Quin cleared his throat. "How is Abuelito?"

Their grandmother looked even more fragile than at the hospital. Deep wrinkles etched across her face and blended with dark shadows beneath her eyes.

"The same. You spoke to your mother?"

They nodded, and her taut shoulders relaxed a little. "I tried not to worry about you two sitting in this house alone. You found something to eat?"

She decided not to mention the cold tortillas and nodded, even though her stomach still felt empty. The twins had packed a candy bar stash in their suitcases anyway, knowing Abuelita wouldn't have any sweets in the house.

"Bueno. I'll say good night." She hesitated like she wanted to say more. Instead, she nodded her head and said, "Buenas noches," closing the door gently behind her.

Pen sighed. La Condesa had never been one to show affection, and she would willingly admit she followed in her grandmother's footsteps, but a hug might have made her feel better.

She paced the floor of their small room, from the large window to the door. Quin rustled around his backpack and pulled out a chocolate bar. "Sustenance." He offered her half. "We have a long night ahead of us."

She took the candy. "We do?" She yawned despite her anxiety over her grandfather and the codex.

"We're the only ones who know why Abuelito was attacked. That means we're the only ones who can find out who did it and how to keep him safe. I thought you wanted to be an investigator."

She stuck her tongue out. "I do. Stop lecturing me and tell me your idea already."

He pulled out the thick file of notes. "Abuelito's been looking for the Codex Cardona for years. Don't you think the answer is somewhere in here?"

Quin spread the notes across the bed. Then he

positioned the Eagle Warrior against the pillow as if the warrior could oversee the entire process.

Pen's phone buzzed and they both jumped. She grabbed the phone. The message flashed up, then mimicked an explosion as it self-destructed. "Archie. He wants to know if we're okay?"

He started riffling through the notes. "We will be."

She nodded, his determination catching. Or maybe the chocolate buoyed her spirit. She added a bag of licorice and a box of fruit candy to the pile of notes on the bed and grabbed her first stick of licorice and the earliest dated note she could find. Now that they had something to do, she felt certain they could solve this mystery. They had to, before somebody else found the codex first.

13

Quin awoke first the next morning. He pulled on yesterday's jeans and rummaged in his suitcase for his Mexico soccer jersey and pulled it over his head.

"Mmm-phh," Pen muttered, her dark hair sticking out from under her pillow. He tiptoed out of the room into the open-air hallway. The tiles were pleasantly chilly on his bare feet and sunlight streamed into the atrium. He crossed the courtyard, the smooth stones under his toes already warming in the sun. When he reached the kitchen door, voices floated out. His heart leaped. Had Abuelito woken up and returned during the night?

He ran the last few steps through the door and skidded to a stop inside the kitchen. A blue flame sputtered on the stove. Abuela held a frying pan over it to heat tortillas. She was dressed in a flowing white skirt and blue shirt with her hair up in her customary loose bun. The shadows under her eyes matched her shirt and his spirits fell even before he saw her visitor. Professor Flores eyed him across a steaming mug of coffee.

"Buenos dias, Quintus." His grandmother flipped the tortilla in the pan with two fingers. "It's about time you were out of bed."

Quin stared, open-mouthed. "What's *he* doing here?"

Professor Flores frowned, but Abuela smiled. "The

professor heard of Miguel's accident and kindly offered to help." She slid the steaming tortillas onto a plate brightly painted with the face of the Aztec sun god and handed it to Quin. "Eat, m'ijo. I felt so guilty you had a cold dinner last night I couldn't leave this morning without giving you a proper breakfast."

He automatically set the plate on the kitchen table and plopped down across from Professor Flores. "How are you going to help us?"

Annoyance flicked across the man's face, but he smoothed his mustache.

"I talked with your mother. I believe we've come to a satisfactory agreement. One that frees your grandmother from worrying about you when she should be with poor Miguel."

Quin stiffened. Professor Flores was having private phone conversations with his mother? About him and Pen? He curled his lip at the professor. "My grandfather's name is Director Reyes."

Professor Flores raised a dark eyebrow and surveyed him with more interest. He took a slow swallow of coffee, made a face, and set the mug down. "Of course. I did not mean to be so forward." He turned to Abuela as he apologized, not to Quin.

"Your offer is so kind. Do not worry about formalities." She waved the apology away.

"What offer?" He felt jumpy, like he did in the last minutes of a game when he had to keep the other team from scoring. Where was Pen? He needed backup now.

His grandmother cleared her throat and sat down in the chair between him and the professor, her back to the sizzling tortillas in the frying pan. "After a lot of thought, your parents and I decided it would be best for all of us if you and your sister were somewhere where you could be looked after."

"You're looking after us." His voice shot up an octave. He gritted his teeth and eyed Professor Flores. The man scooped another spoonful of instant coffee into his mug and stirred the dark granules until they dissolved, turning the coffee a deep black.

"M'ijo, I cannot continue to—" Abuela's voice caught and she put one hand to her mouth and closed her eyes. Quin had never seen her like this. La Condesa was as strong and unwavering as a Spanish conquistador, as composed as the Queen of Spain.

The old lady took a deep breath and opened her eyes. She reached out and brushed her hand across his. Her fingertips left small trails of tortilla mix on his hand like the ruins of an ancient village. He studied his grandmother's hand, slightly yellowed by the mix and more wrinkled than he remembered. It reminded him of the painting of the tortilla maker stolen from Abuelito's drawer. He looked up and found the same quiet strength of the Aztec woman in his grandmother's eyes.

"They don't allow children in Miguel's room at the hospital," Abuela said. "I need to be there for the moment when he awakens. The doctor doesn't know how long it will be." Again, her voice swelled, but she managed to continue. "Your mother and I agree it would be better not to leave you and Pen alone in this house all summer."

"All summer? But Abuelito will wake up soon." To make himself believe it, he said it again. "Abuelito will wake up."

Professor Flores tsked and made a sympathetic face at Abuela. Quin's blood heated up like a tortilla in a pan.

"We don't know when he will awake," Abuela said softly. "Maybe today and maybe…" She didn't finish.

Professor Flores reached out to pat her hand. "I've spoken in detail with Maria."

He bristled at the professor's familiar use of his mother's name.

"We've decided it's best for you and your sister to meet Maria in Spain. She has managed to rearrange her schedule." The professor's face soured. "Your father is also working on a flight to Spain."

"Spain? We're going to Spain?"

Professor Flores nodded. "To keep you out of your grandmother's way."

The knot in his stomach loosened a little. He hated to leave Abuelito and Abuela, but at least they would be with Mamá and Dad. "Okay, Pen and I have flown alone before."

The professor snorted. "Don't be absurd. How could we worry your beautiful grandmother with that, let alone Maria? I will accompany you. We will all go to Spain together."

He stared at Professor Flores, stunned. He had no retort, no way to see this coming. If this were a game, the professor had just booted the ball into the goal and won. And the man knew it. When Abuela turned back to the stove to get the tortillas, he gave Quin a mocking smile.

His shoulders slumped, and he stared at his plate. Beneath the tortillas, the Aztec god stared angrily at him. The sun god demanded sacrifices, he remembered. He felt like he'd just become one of its victims, helpless to change his destiny.

"No, absolutamente no." Pen stood at the door, her cheeks flushed and hair tangled and sticking up like a bizarre headdress. Her eyes burned with the intensity of a sacrificial fire and she aimed their heat at Professor Flores. "I will not go anywhere with you."

Quin's dad had a term for this type of anger. He called it, El Fuego. When angry, their mother had the ability to melt anything and anyone in her path, Adam Grey explained once to the twins, so it was better not to be in that path. Pen had inherited every bit of their mother's fire, and she held her own when she threw one of her famous Penstorms.

She held her gaze and Quin, between her and the professor, melted in its heat. Even Professor Flores wilted a little. He tried to smile.

"I remember when your mother had such a temper. She made a similar statement once. She eventually came around."

She glared at the man and Quin thought she might actually hit him, but Abuela stepped between them and waved her wooden spatula in the air.

"Basta, Penelope! That's enough." She straightened her shoulders and squared up to Pen, the stoop in her back disappearing. The sunlight shining through the open window turned her hair into a shimmering silver halo. Her gaze, as fierce as the Eagle Warrior's, took in both twins.

"Niños, sometimes in life we must do things we do not want with people we do not like. This is one of those times." She held their gaze, daring either twin to oppose her. His sister didn't get El Fuego from Mamá, he thought. It came straight from La Condesa.

Pen crossed her arms and gave Abuela a look usually reserved for the opposing team and Mamá. "You'll send us halfway around the world with a stranger?" She looked at Quin for help. He stared at his uneaten tortillas.

"I've known José Luis many years," Abuela replied calmly. "He's been a friend of your mother's since college, and more recently, your grandfather. I trust him to deliver you safely to Maria."

"Do not blame the girl too much, Inez," Professor Flores said to La Condesa. "She's upset and at this age, girls are prone to emotional outbursts."

"I'll show you emotional outbursts—"

Quin cut her off quickly. "When are we leaving?"

"Tonight," Abuela said.

"Tonight?" both twins cried out at the same time.

"Of course," Professor Flores said. "We must free Inez to be at Miguel's side."

The twins stared at each other in dismay.

"Come eat breakfast, m'ija. You'll feel better," Abuela said.

"I've lost my appetite." Pen glared at Professor Flores, then included Quin in the heat. "I suppose you'll do whatever they tell you to."

His cheeks reddened, and he gave her a pleading look.

"We don't have a choice," he mumbled.

"You must understand," Abuela began, but Pen spun away and walked out of the kitchen.

He dropped his gaze to his plate, where the Aztec mocked him behind a half-eaten tortilla. *That's right,* his cold eyes said. *Hold still while I tear out your still beating heart.* Quin gritted his teeth. If he had been an Aztec sacrifice all those years ago, would he have climbed quietly up the temple stairs to his death, or would he have fought for life? Where was his fuego? Why was his sister the only one with any fire inside her?

Pen slammed the heavy wooden door of her bedroom with a satisfying bang that rattled the room and sent a fine layer of dust wafting down from the ceiling. She tried to fight off the tears, but she still hadn't cried for Abuelito. It was too much. She threw herself on the unmade bed, ashamed that she felt more upset about traveling with Professor Flores than she had about her grandfather's attack.

This is Mamá's fault, Pen thought, choking back a sob. While Abuelito lay in a hospital bed, she'd be shuffled off to another country with a near stranger—one she couldn't stand, let alone trust—all because it was more convenient for Mamá.

She was never one to cry for long. When she finished, she sat up and rubbed her eyes.

"Feel better?" Quin asked, startling her so much she nearly fell backwards off the bed.

"Ahh!" she shouted. She regained her balance and glared at her brother. "Thanks for the support. It's like you want to go to Spain with him."

He took his glasses off and rubbed at a spot. "It's not that. Of course I'd rather be here." He slid the frames back on, magnifying his eyes, and blinked at her. "Arguing was pointless. You know how La Condesa is once she's made up her mind, not to mention Mamá."

Pen sighed and bit her lip. She knew better than anyone how difficult the Reyes women could be. But she wasn't quite ready to forgive Quin. He must have sensed this. He walked over to the desk and picked up a plate she hadn't noticed.

"Cheese quesadillas?" He held out the plate. It was a peace offering, and the chocolate bar and licorice from the night before had long since worn off. Pen sighed and took the plate. She couldn't stay mad at him for long. He was her only ally now, and more importantly, her partner in the investigation.

While she ate, he filled her in on the details of their impending trip. Professor Flores left after she stormed out of the kitchen, saying he had errands to attend to. He would meet the children at the airport. Abuela had left for the hospital. The twins were to stay at the house until this afternoon, then call a taxi and stop by the hospital before heading to the airport.

"They've got it all figured out." Pen set down the plate and chewed slowly, the corn tortillas and queso fresco losing their taste. She traced the designs around the Aztec god's face. The nuns at St. Mary's would call this an idol, and the Aztecs savages for killing thousands of people in bloody sacrifices. The plate's empty eyes haunted her, the same eyes as the Eagle Warrior and Camila. *Help us*, they cried. Were they the same eyes that convinced Bernardino de Sahagún to spend sixty years away from his home in Spain, working with the Aztec people and creating painted books to record their history?

She hadn't been away from home five days and a rush of longing swept through her. Why couldn't they be in Boston right now, with soccer camp and Michael Blalock, and Mamá and Dad, with Abuela and Abuelito here the way they were supposed to be, and nobody hurt and no mystery to solve. She blew out a puff of air. Pen didn't think investigating would be so hard. She turned their client's last email over in her mind. The words "in danger" kept jumping out at her. A shiver ran through her. What was the danger? Would it go away if they left? Or would it still threaten their grandparents? She turned to her brother to tell him they were done investigating, but he was already pulling on his backpack.

"We have most of the day to figure out who attacked Abuelito. Don't we have a meeting to make?"

"You mean you're not going to stay here like La Condesa asked?" She eyed him doubtfully.

Quin shook his head, his eyes bright. "I only promised her we would stop by the hospital before going to the airport. I implied the rest."

Pen grinned, forgetting her doubts. "The café is near Abuelito's museum," she pointed out. "We could stop by and look at his office."

"What for? The thief already took the tortilla maker, and nobody knows about the Eagle Warrior." He patted his backpack, where the warrior was tucked inside.

"I don't know," she admitted. "But that's where Abuelito was attacked and where he kept his information on the Codex Cardona until he gave it to us. Maybe there's something there that will help us figure out what's going on."

She pulled on her sneakers and ran to the door, stopping when she realized Quin hadn't followed. "What?"

"You might want to comb your hair first." He gestured around his own head. "But Michael Blalock isn't here, so maybe it doesn't matter."

Pen shrieked and ripped off one of her shoes, pitching it at his head. He ducked out of the way, then hurried past her.

"Just wait until I tell Anna you talk about her in your sleep," she shouted after him, then dove under the bed to search for her misguided shoe.

14

Abuelito's secretary clucked sympathetically when the twins explained they wanted to see their grandfather's office.

"I understand you're upset but the police say it's a crime scene. I'm not supposed to let anyone inside."

"But we're not just anyone." Not Pen's best argument, Quin thought, but they were pressed for time.

The secretary bit her lip and sighed. She hadn't put eye makeup on and nothing distracted from her bloodshot eyes. Perhaps they weren't the only ones affected by the attack.

"Por favor," she pleaded. "We just want to see if...if Abuelito left his phone there."

"We won't touch anything," he promised.

The secretary glanced down the hallway at passing tourists and rubbed her eyes. "I've been on the phone all morning canceling the fiesta. I could use a break." She led them to the office, checked the hall once more, and opened the door. "Un minuto, no más."

They stepped inside and looked around. The office appeared unchanged. The computer screen was still blank. The stacks of files appeared untouched.

"I thought the police said the office was ransacked," Quin muttered.

"It always looks that way," Pen said.

He nodded. They walked around the desk. From what he could see, nothing was disturbed. If whoever had attacked Abuelito had been looking for something, he'd hidden his tracks well—not that it would be hard to do amongst the usual clutter.

The secretary rapped on the door. "Niños? Time to go. We don't want the police to find us here."

Pen sighed and walked to the door. "Maybe we'll learn something from our client." She checked her watch. "We have to get to the café."

Quin looked around slowly. He'd learned through art that you had to paint a little at a time in order to see the whole picture. Maybe there was a piece here he was missing.

"Children?" The secretary stuck her head inside the door, her brows furrowed. "Por favor, we must go."

"Or course." Pen stepped through the door, forcing the secretary to step back, buying her brother a few more seconds to look around.

He walked out seconds later. "Gracias." He grabbed her arm and pulled her down the hall.

"What is it?" she asked, but he didn't slow down until they emerged from the museum and ran down the steps.

Pen finally stopped. "What did you see?"

Quin shook his head. "It's what I didn't see." He pulled her forward and they started walking again. Café Azteca was down the street.

"O-kay. "What didn't you see?"

"The giant head. It's gone."

Pen squinted at him. "We didn't even go past the giant heads. And they're too big to carry--"

"No." He hopped impatiently from one foot to the other. Usually, she was faster to catch on, but she'd never held much interest in the giant heads unless she was teasing him. "The little one that sits on Abuelito's desk. The one that laughs at me—" Quin stopped, embarrassed. Pen raised an eyebrow, but she didn't interrupt.

"It's not there. I looked on the other shelves, the floor. I even opened the drawers and searched there."

"Rulebreaker." She sounded delighted. "But I don't see what that tells us. So what if it's gone? What does a fake giant head have to do with Abuelito or the Codex Cardona?"

Quin wasn't used to this role. He waited just long enough to make her cry out. "Quin-tus! Tell me or I'll tell Anna you like her."

"I do not." He decided it was better to tell her everything, though. "That head sits on the desk near Abuelito. You can't get to it without going all the way around the desk."

He paused to catch his breath. Even though Mexico City sat in a valley, the altitude was higher than he was used to. She looked like she wanted to strangle him, but she kept her hands balled into fists by her side.

"What does it mean?"

"It means either Abuelito surprised the attacker in his office," he said, "which means the attacker got behind the desk before he came inside, panicked when Abuelito surprised him, and grabbed the closest thing to him to use as a weapon."

"The giant head," Pen said thoughtfully. "You might be right."

Quin shook his head. "I don't think that's what happened, though. Abuelito was hit on the back of the head. If he walked into the office, he would have been facing the attacker unless he tried to run away."

"Abuelito doesn't run away."

"No. He's like you and Mamá."

Her face darkened. "Oh no," she whispered. "Abuelito was sitting at his desk when it happened. He let his attacker walk up behind him."

He nodded, strangely relieved his sister now knew what he did.

"Abuelito knew his attacker."

Outside Café Azteca, Quin pulled the red scarf out of his backpack and handed it Pen. She tied it around her neck and resettled her dark hair around it. "How do I look?" she asked, fidgeting with the scarf's loose ends.

Her brother scrutinized her. "Like Mamá. That scarf is something she would wear."

She blushed, pleased, but then bit her lip. She couldn't forget Mamá was sending them to Spain with Professor Flores. "Okay," she said, trying to sound fearless. "Let's go in."

They ducked out of the bright morning sunshine into the dim cafe. It took a few moments for her eyes to adjust to the shadowy light. At mid-morning, the restaurant was mostly empty, its small wooden tables separated into sections by woven bamboo screens. Huge ceiling fans turned slowly, stirring the scent of coffee in lazy swirls. Banana trees in oversized clay pots decorated the entryway. She noted the Aztec designs on their sides. Now that they were searching for the Codex Cardona, she saw Aztec influence everywhere they went, something she normally wouldn't have paid any attention to.

She stepped behind one of the banana trees to survey the customers. Quin gave her an odd look and continued to stand in full view of anyone in the café. Pen sighed. She guessed the point of this meeting was to be seen. She stepped out beside her brother.

Lunch wouldn't be served for another two hours, so the café held only a few stragglers from breakfast. Delicious smells wafted out of the kitchen and her stomach growled at the spicy aroma.

Two middle-aged woman sat nearby, sipping coffee and laughing loudly. An elderly man read a paper, one hand curled protectively around his cup. Two waiters chatted at the bar, barely glancing at the children before going back to their discussion.

Pen felt her heart sink. Had their client failed to show again? Then Quin tugged her elbow and pointed to the back corner of the café. Bamboo screens nearly shielded a few tables from view. A woman sat in the farthest chair, and she was watching them.

"That must be our client," she said, "unless it's the old guy reading the newspaper."

His eyes were closed, and his head bent over the newspaper as he dozed. "He doesn't look like someone in danger," he muttered.

They wove through the tables and approached the woman.

"Pen, it's her," Quin whispered as they reached the last table.

"Who?" she whispered back, not recognizing the shadowy figure. Then the woman stood, and Pen understood. This was the woman her brother had flattened at the zoo.

"You're the Spanish coin lady," he said, just as the woman said, "The children from the zoo."

They stared at each other. The woman reached for her throat and Pen mirrored the movement and touched the red scarf around hers.

"You're P and Q?" Her hand moved to cover her mouth. "I hired children to find the codex?" she whispered. "Oh no. What have I done?"

15

Angela—for that was their client's name—bought the twins café con leche and muttered to herself while they waited for the drinks.

"Who are you?" Pen finally burst out. "You hired us to look for—"

"Shh. Don't say it." Her eyes roamed the nearly empty restaurant, causing Quin to do the same.

"You hired us to find a painted book," she whispered. "Why?"

The woman played with her phone, tapping buttons and turning it over and over in her hands. She had medium-length, wavy brown hair she kept pushing back behind her ears. Her brown eyes might be friendly, Quin thought, if they weren't full of fear. She didn't look too much older than Archie. The Spanish accent that made Professor Flores sound silly flowed smoothly off her tongue.

"It was a shortcut," Angela said as the drinks arrived. "A mistake." The waiter set two steaming mugs down. "I should never have contacted you."

"But you did," he said. "And we're involved now."

"And you may not know this, but our grandfather's in the hospital and somehow, it's all related to the co—the painted book," Pen amended. "And we have to go to Spain tonight so please, if you know anything about it—anything that could help our grandfather—tell us now."

Angela sat up straight and put the phone on the table. "Your grandfather's in the hospital? You're going to Spain? Tonight?"

The twins exchanged miserable looks. "We have to," Quin said. "Our grandmother's making us so she can take care of Abuelito."

"What happened to your grandfather?" she asked. Her toe tapped the floor, rattling the table and sloshing their drinks

"What makes you think something happened to him?"

"Pen," he interrupted, surprised by his sister's rude tone. Angela was their client, after all. "Our grandfather's—"

"Sick," Pen interrupted. "Very sick."

"I'm sorry to hear that." She hesitated, then said, "My mother's ill, too." She took a quick gulp of coffee. Her eyes never moved from the door. The two women got up and walked out. The old man had woken up and continued to read his paper, and the waiters had disappeared into the kitchen.

"You said you're going to Spain?" Angela asked.

"We leave tonight," Quin confirmed.

"With Professor Flores, the worst escort in the world," his sister groaned.

"Professor Flores? You know him?" Angela stared back and forth at the twins, her eyes wide.

"Do you?" both twins asked.

"I work with him. Well, I'm a graduate student in art history. Professor Flores has been helping me with my graduate project."

"The Codex Cardona," Pen said.

"No," Angela shook her head, her cheeks turning pink. "It has nothing to do with that, but I've heard he speaks about the codex many times. It's intriguing to think about this ancient painted book floating around the world somewhere, waiting to be discovered."

Angela sounded a little like Mamá, captivated by the idea of unearthing part of history. Quin sipped his cafe con leche.

"So you decided to look for it, too?" he asked.

Angela hesitated, then nodded. "I noticed some notes and sketches in the professor's office one day and—"

"You snooped around," Pen said.

"Yes," she admitted. "But the paintings were curious. I'd never seen anything quite like them. I learned they were pages from a lost painted book the professor was searching for. He was corresponding with an art director in Mexico City—"

"Abuelito," Quin said.

Their companion's mouth made an 'O.' "Your grandfather's the director?" Her face drained of color and for the first time, she looked away from the door and down at her hands. "So he's not sick. He's—"

"Going to make it," he said fiercely, surprising himself.

Pen nodded. "How did you know what happened to Abuelito?" she asked.

"It was all over the news," Angela murmured. "The museum director attacked in his office." Then she covered her face with her hands. "What was I thinking?"

"Please," Quin begged. "Can you tell us more about the codex? We don't have much time."

Angela sighed heavily. "I started researching Mexican painted books, but I couldn't find much. It's like it appeared out of thin air one day and disappeared the next."

"Lost," his sister muttered. He nodded, thinking about Abuelito's lost friend.

"What?" the woman asked.

"How did you get the Eagle Warrior?" Pen asked. "The one you gave us?"

"I borrowed it from Professor Flores."

"I can't believe he let you," Quin said, thinking how protective the professor was of his possessions.

Angela's cheeks turned red. "He didn't. I sort of, um—"

"Oh, you stole it," Pen said.

"Only for one night." Angela clasped her hands together as if pleading for the children to understand. "I was going to return it the next morning, but I didn't have the chance. He started asking me odd questions."

"That's normal for him," Pen muttered.

"What kind of questions?" Quin asked.

"Had I seen paintings of Aztecs around his office? Did I notice anybody suspicious-looking snooping around?"

He suspected Angela didn't think of herself as someone suspicious.

"Then he shooed me away. That was the last time I saw him. He didn't come to my graduate lecture. The department secretary felt sorry for me and let it slip that he'd come here, instead. I decided to follow him, and on a whim, I did a web search for anyone looking for the codex or ancient artifacts."

"And you found our website," Pen finished. She beamed.

Angela sighed. "I thought if I could find the codex first, Professor Flores wouldn't be so angry when I returned the page I took from him."

Quin took another sip of the café con leche. It was creamy but bitter. He grabbed a packet of brown sugar and dumped it into the cup. "Do you think Professor Flores is working with Abuelito to find the codex?"

It was hard to imagine their grandfather and the professor in league together, but if Abuelito had been obsessed with the Cardona for years and Professor Flores, too…how well did he know his grandfather?

"Maybe," Pen said. "Abuela did say Professor Flores had been in contact with Abuelito lately."

"And why would he have been at the bookshop yesterday unless he already knew what someone sent to him?" Quin said.

"Excuse me," Angela said, "Do you mean the painting at

the bookshop? I thought it was stolen?"

"How do you know about that?" his sister asked.

Angela shrugged. "I sort of followed the professor. I wasn't sure where to go after I ran into you at the zoo. By the way, can I have my scarf back?"

Pen untied the scarf and handed it across the table. "Why didn't you meet us at the zoo and tell us this?"

"I thought I was in danger," The art student slipped the scarf around her neck and looped it deftly into a complex knot that lay flat against her white blouse.

"I wasn't sure if anyone was following me, and I wanted to see what you looked like. I've never hired private investigators before."

Quin blinked. Private investigators. He thought of the website. Yes, international agents of intrigue did imply they were private investigators.

"Did you run into me on purpose at the zoo?" he asked.

"No. I didn't realize who you were. I thought you'd picked the scarf up by mistake. The man following you—"

"The man in the red hat," Pen said excitedly. "I told you he was following us," she told him.

"Actually, I thought he was who I was hiring, but when I saw him take the envelope from you at the bookshop, I changed my mind."

"You saw him!" his sister shouted. "Who is he?"

"Shh." Angela leaned in toward the twins. "I think he followed me from Spain."

Her words caused them to pause and glance around the cafe. A waiter greeted another customer at the door. The man took a seat near the front of the café and ordered coffee. He took out his phone and started playing with it.

"Why?" Pen whispered, turning back to Angela. "How could he know about the codex?"

"How could he know about us?" Quin murmured, only loud enough for his twin to hear.

"I don't know," their companion said. "But after your grandfather was attacked, my hotel room was broken into and what little information I had on the codex was stolen." She rummaged in her purse. "And I found this note." She laid a torn piece of paper on the table. They leaned forward to read it.

Stop searching for the painted book, or the curse will find you, too.

The twins exchanged a look. They didn't mention that Abuelito's painting had been stolen, or that they'd received their own warning about the curse. Goosebumps raised the hair on his arms. He tried to hide his nervousness by taking another sip of his drink.

"I'm sorry I got you into this," Angela said. "I should never have taken the painting off Professor Flores' desk, or followed him to Mexico City, or—" she grimaced at the twins and sighed. "Or hired you two. I did think you would be—"

She didn't say older, though clearly that's what she'd expected. What any normal person would expect, Quin thought.

Angela opened her purse and took out the same Spanish coins she'd spilled at the zoo. "Here, you said you were going to Spain. Let me give you something for your trouble. It's not the money I promised you but—"

"You can't pay us. We haven't solved the case," Pen said. "We don't know who took the envelope from Quin—"

"Or why he attacked Abuelito, if he did," Quin added.

Angela shook her head. "This is too dangerous to continue." She snapped the purse shut. "In fact, you should tell the police about all of this."

"Will you?" Pen challenged.

The woman drew back like a child caught stealing candy. "No. Professor Flores can't know of my involvement. He— I-I'm sorry," she finished. "There is no more case. I'm going home."

"To Spain?" his sister asked. "Maybe we could meet—"

"No," Angela said. "I'm done with this. So are you. You're finished with this investigation. Do you understand?"

Pen sat back, a sullen expression on her face. She hated to be told she was finished with anything. The woman stood, tugged once at the scarf, and started to walk away but turned back.

"Professor Flores isn't a bad man. Please don't mention any of this to him."

"But if you think this is dangerous, aren't you worried he's in danger, too?" Pen asked.

Angela hesitated, and her large brown eyes filled with tears. "I'm worried about all of us. Good-bye P and Q." She turned and walked quickly out of the café.

16

They returned to the empty house, both jumpy after Angela's tale. Pen grabbed Abuela's cast iron skillet from the kitchen and the twins tiptoed through every room, but the house was as empty as they'd left it.

They returned to their room and she set the skillet on her bed.

"I guess we better pack," Quin said. She eyed him across the room. His clothes were already placed neatly in his suitcase. He clearly meant she should pack. Hers lay on top of her bed. Instead, she flipped open her laptop, deciding to check her email one last time. Of course, now that they knew Angela was their client, there wouldn't be an email from her. The way she fled the cafe, Pen didn't think they'd hear from her again.

Maybe Michael had written something that would cheer her up, though she couldn't imagine what could make her feel better about Abuelito and having to fly to Spain with Professor Flores. When she opened her inbox, she frowned, puzzled.

"We have another message from the website."

"From Angela? What does it say?" Quin sat on his bed and tapped his sneakers on the tile floor.

Pen gasped and reread the words on her screen, unable to believe them at first. Slowly, she read them out loud.

A book with no pages is but a lie. Some stories, like old men, simply must die. Leave the Codex Cardona alone or the curse will find you, too.

Both twins remained silent, the words sinking in.

"This isn't from Angela," Pen finally said.

"Then who's it from?" Quin came over to read the words on the screen. The computer glare reflected off his glasses.

"Die," he whispered. "Curse."

She typed rapidly on the computer, then shook her head. "It's just a random email address. I can trace it to the mail client, but even that won't tell us who sent it. Anyone can set up an email address and use it once."

The computer began to ring, startling them both. *Call from Archie* popped up on the screen. She clicked to accept almost without thinking. Their brother's face filled the frame. His dark hair and eyes matched Pen's more than Quin's. He grinned at them.

"Hey, I wanted to catch you before your flight, and this way I can see you, since I don't have video capability on Odyssey yet." Then he frowned. "What's wrong? You both look pale. Not getting enough sun down there? Is that even possible?"

"Abuelito's in the hospital," Quin said.

Archie nodded. "Sorry, you're right. Of course you're worried. So am I. Especially after hearing Mamá's plan to send you to Spain."

Pen's hopes lifted. "So you think it's loco, too, right?"

"Completely. You two are old enough to take care of yourselves, but there's no telling Mamá that."

The doorbell rang. "The taxi." Quin sighed. "We have to go."

Archie leaned into the camera so it magnified his nose and dark eyes. He didn't look like the heartthrob girls thought he was now, just their dork of an older brother. "Okay. I just wanted to tell you to have a good trip. What is it Mamá always tells you? Mind your P's and Q's?"

Pen rolled her eyes. The last thing they needed was someone else telling them what to do. "We'll be fine," she snapped. "Just flying across the world while Abuelito is in the hospital and everyone else is too busy to care."

He leaned back. "Tranquila, Pen, you know I'm joking. I'm sorry about this mess, for real."

"Not sorry enough to offer to fly down and be with us," she snapped.

A look of guilt crossed his face and he swept a hand through his dark hair. "I can't leave now. I have class and I can't miss my labs. And my internship is—"

"It's okay," Quin said. "We know everyone's busy."

"You know I'd be there if I could. But hey, at least we have Odyssey." He leaned into the camera so close only one eye and nostril could be seen. "Don't forget, Big Brother's watching," he said in such a creepy tone even Pen barely held in a giggle.

The horn blasted again outside the house and she remembered they had to leave to catch a flight to Spain with her least favorite person in the world besides—perhaps—Eileen Esposito. Without saying goodbye, she slammed the laptop shut. Her last view of her older brother was of Archie with his mouth hanging open. Yeah, some heartbreaker he was.

"Pen," Quin protested. He started throwing her clothes into her suitcase. "This isn't Archie's fault."

Pen glowered at him. She reluctantly grabbed the rest of her clothes and shoved them on top of the others, then slammed the suitcase shut. "We don't need them since they obviously don't need us. And we have something bigger to think about. Who sent us that message? Who else knows about the Codex Cardona?"

"No one else knew about the codex but us and Abuelito." Quin picked up his own suitcase and staggered to the desk for his backpack. He unzipped it and Pen saw him check the envelope that held the Aztec Warrior painting.

"That's not true." She yanked the suitcase off the bed. It thudded to the floor. "Professor Flores does."

He gaped at her. "You don't mean he sent us the message?"

"Who else?"

"But how could he know we're investigating? And why would he say that stuff?"

"How did he know we were going to the bookshop?" Pen asked. "And isn't it convenient that he volunteered to take us to Spain? And he's gotten to know Abuelito so well through his research? We already know he's looking for the Codex Cardona. What if he decided he wanted to find it himself instead of with Abuelito?"

Her cheeks were flushed, and she took short, rapid breaths. "And now we're flying all the way to Spain with him."

"Mamá wouldn't send us with Professor Flores if she didn't trust him."

"Mamá's not here," she cried. And then she was crying and stamping her foot because she hated crying.

Her phone dinged, and she sniffed and slid it from her pocket.

α : I'm sorry.

Pen swallowed her remorse for how she'd treated Archie. She started to type back, then stopped. No, he could have stepped in somehow and kept them from being sent to Spain. He could have flown there.

She shoved the phone in her pocket just as the horn blasted a third time. She wiped her tears with her shirt sleeve and took a deep breath. Quin swung his backpack on his back. "Still, it wouldn't hurt to keep our eyes on Professor Flores."

"All the way to Spain," Pen whispered.

After a hurried goodbye at the hospital, the taxi driver dropped the twins off at the airport. They found Professor

Flores at the check-in counter, haggling for a seat in business class.

"So that's one seat in business class and two in coach." The man at the counter typed into his computer. "Bueno, I have your reservations and here are your boarding passes."

He handed the twins their passes with a smirk.

"Figures," Pen whispered. "Of course he wouldn't upgrade our seats."

"At least we'll be far away from him for the flight," Quin whispered back.

"Stop whispering and keep up," the professor snapped. "I'll not miss my flight because of children."

She rolled her eyes and they ran after Professor Flores. He was already through the metal detector at the security gate and a guard had his rolling suitcase open as he searched the contents.

Quin hefted his backpack into the security conveyer belt and passed through the detector. As the backpack slid out the other end, a guard stepped forward and picked it up.

"I need to check the contents."

He sighed and watched the guard pull out his camera, colored pencils, sketch pad and book on Mexican art. The folder with Abuelito's notes slid out with it and Quin stiffened. The Eagle Warrior.

The guard put the camera back down and flipped open the file folder, flicking past the yellowed notes. He stopped when he saw the Eagle Warrior, cocked his head, and pointed to it.

"Nice painting," he said. "Did you do it?"

He shook his head mutely. The guard closed the folder and gestured for him to move along. He sighed with relief, glad most people couldn't recognize four-hundred-year-old art when it was staring them in the face. Behind him, a guard examined Pen's electronics, from her laptop to her smartphone. Another one forced Professor Flores to dump the entire contents of his carry-on bag onto a counter. She examined each item carefully, holding up a pair of colorful silk underwear, and raised her eyebrows at Professor Flores.

Quin snorted and glanced back at Pen to share in the joke, but she was still stuffing her laptop into her bag and giving the guard a look that said he'd better not ask her to do anything else.

"That's a gift," the professor said, and Quin turned back to him. "A tourist's replica, nothing more."

Quin barely stifled a gasp, turning it into a cough at the last moment. Professor Flores flicked him an irritated look and he looked away.

"Por favor," the Spaniard drew out the word. "We must go or we will miss the flight." He gestured to the twins. The guard's eyes followed, and her hard stare softened.

"Bueno," she said. "You may go. Next time pack your souvenirs in your checked luggage, or they may be confiscated. That underwear, too," she added, and flashed a smile at the twins.

Splotches of red mottled the professor's face and throat. He said nothing but threw his items into his bag and zipped it furiously.

"What's this about underwear?" his sister asked

Quin was no longer in the mood to joke. "Never mind," he whispered. "Professor Flores has—"

"Niños!" the man shouted, his anger now directed at them. "Ya vamos."

"Oh good, he's only speaking Spanish now," Pen said sarcastically. "I'm glad he upgraded to business class. I don't want to look at his oily face any longer."

Quin stumbled behind her, his mind still numb at what he'd seen. "Pen, we can't get on the plane," he mumbled. "We can't go with him." He dragged his feet to the gate.

She turned and walked backward, still moving as the professor requested but able to blast him with the entirety of her exasperation.

"You're saying that now? Where were you when I was arguing with La Condesa in the kitchen?"

He felt his face redden. He'd let her down by not backing her earlier. "But," he protested, "we can't trust Professor Flores."

Pen rolled her eyes and backed into another traveler. "Perdón," she muttered, barely looking at the older woman she'd bumped into.

The woman glared at them both and turned to her husband, declaring loudly in English, "Don't children have any manners?"

His sister whirled toward her, ready to launch into a tirade. Quin gripped her arm like a soccer ball and jerked her away.

"Forget her. I have to tell you something."

"Now boarding all rows for Madrid," a woman chimed over the intercom. Professor Flores shouted at them to hurry. He already stood at the gate.

"What do you think he'd do if we missed the flight?" Pen asked, slowing her steps.

"Penelope Grey Reyes, listen to me."

Her eyes widened, and she stopped in her tracks. He only called his twin Penelope when he wanted to make her mad or he was dead serious. "What is it?"

Quin swallowed hard. "It's Professor Flores. He has the giant head."

"Last call for Madrid," the voice chimed. "Now boarding all rows." The professor waited in the boarding tunnel, fury written across his face.

"The giant head from Abuelito's desk?"

"Yes." He explained as quickly as he could. "I saw it in his bag at the security check. He's taking it to Spain to get it away from here. Don't you see?"

Pen bit her lip and stared at him. It was rare that he had his sister's undivided attention.

"It's the perfect weapon. Professor Flores used it to hit Abuelito on the head and now he's taking the evidence to

Spain so the police can't arrest him. He—"

Quin stopped talking. Professor Flores' hand clamped down on Pen's shoulder and spun her around.

"I'm beginning to regret my decision to help Maria. Are you deaf? They've asked us to board three times now." He pushed Pen ahead of him none too gently and reached out for him. He ducked under his arm and dashed to his twin's side.

"Pen," he tried to whisper, but it came out as more of a squeak. Then he took a step away. She looked like Mamá before she yelled at them for playing soccer in the back-yard instead of finishing their homework—no, like La Con-desa when the twins hadn't finished their chores. No, he amended once more. Like an Eagle Warrior in her own right, her face dark and furious and proud all at once.

She handed her boarding pass to the attendant.

"But we can't go," he whispered, shooting Professor Flo-res a look to make sure he wasn't eavesdropping. The pro-fessor slapped his boarding pass against his hand, clearly annoyed, but his eyes were on the pretty flight attendant at the gate.

Pen leveled Quin with a gaze so forceful he knew right away she'd made up her mind.

"If everything you say is true, then Spain is exactly where I'm going. I'm going to find out what he did to Abuelito." The attendant returned her boarding pass and held out her hand for Quin's.

She turned and raised her eyebrows, an unspoken ques-tion passing between them. He again felt the rush of shame that she even had to ask. She wouldn't have if he'd only spoken up in the kitchen when Professor Flores suggested this preposterous idea.

"Of course I'm going with you." He handed his pass to the attendant. "Someone has to make sure you stay out of trouble."

"Good," she whispered. "Because our case just got a lot more dangerous."

17

Professor Flores stopped in business class and directed the children to find their seats in coach.

"That figures," Quin complained as they stowed their bags beneath the seats in front of them. They were on the last row, in front of the toilets, which meant their seats wouldn't recline on the overnight flight and they had to watch a steady parade of intestinally challenged passengers hurry by them. Not to mention the smell.

Pen settled into the window seat farthest from the lavatories and pressed her nose against the glass, leaving a smudge mark. She rubbed it away, reminded of Professor Flores. "Well, at least we don't have to sit next to him."

The seats continued to fill until the two rows in front of them held a family of young children and frazzled parents. Pen sighed. They wouldn't get much sleep on the flight. She turned to her brother.

"If Professor Flores attacked Abuelito—"

"Shh," her brother whispered. The mother in front of them glanced their direction. She stared curiously at the twins, probably wondering where their parents were, then turned back when one of her children started crying.

"If he attacked Abuelito," Pen whispered, "why would he agree to take us to Spain and meet Mamá?"

Quin frowned. "He didn't get what he wanted," he said

slowly. "If he attacked Abuelito, he must want more information on the Codex Cardona. He's trying to find it, too."

"So he tried to beat us to the bookstore, and then ransacked Abuelito's office, but he didn't find anything."

"Because we have the Eagle Warrior," Quin said. "And Abuelito gave us his notes, too."

"It makes sense." Pen wrinkled her nose as the toilet door opened and closed again. She wondered if Professor Flores had requested these seats for them. "And he's been inside our grandparents' house before, so he would have known exactly where Abeulito's office is. He took Camila—I mean, the tortilla maker painting."

The airplane shook as it gathered speed for takeoff. The force pushed the twins back in their seats. She thought about Professor Flores' appearance in the bookshop. Obviously, he'd suspected Abuelito would receive a page from the codex. Who was sending them? From where? And did he know where the codex was? Pen sighed. Too many unanswered questions, all while their grandfather's attacker sat in business class eating peanuts.

As soon as the plane leveled off, Quin grabbed his backpack and pulled out the folder with the notes. "Maybe we can find something in here that will tell us what Professor Flores knows and why Abuelito was working with him," he said, as if reading her mind. He flipped it open and the Eagle Warrior glared fiercely at them. She wished they had an Eagle Warrior with them to take on the professor.

"Hello," a bubbly voice said. A flight attendant beamed down at them. The cream scarf around her neck reminded Pen of Angela. She wondered if the grad student had flown home yet.

"I'm Camila."

"Really?" She felt like she'd just gotten a sign from the tortilla maker. *Don't give up!*

"I spoke with your tío in business class?" Camila continued.

"Tío?" Quin asked.

Camila cocked her head slightly. "Your uncle José Luis? He asked me to watch over you."

Pen choked on her words. "He's—not—our—uncle."

Camila's broad smile faltered a little. "Oh, are you okay? I assumed he—"

"We're fine." She recovered quickly. "He's our step-mom's brother and our parents are divorcing. They're sending us to Spain to get us out of the way while they fight."

"I'm so sorry." Camila patted Quin's shoulder. "Let me know if there's anything I can do for you. I know," she said, her bright mood returning. "Extra dessert for your meals."

Pen grinned, obviously recovered from her emotional fit. "That'd be great. Extra sodas, too. It takes my mind off our situation." She tipped her chin down and managed to look slightly pitiful.

Quin rolled his eyes after the woman walked away. "Overdoing it, aren't you?"

"I didn't want her to think we'd been kidnapped. We have to get to Spain and figure out why Professor Flores attacked Abuelito and who has the codex. We just have to make it through this flight, first."

"At least we get extra snacks."

She nearly rolled her eyes. Why was her brother always thinking about food? "Did you notice her name is Camila?" She raised her eyebrows at him. "Maybe the painted book isn't cursed. Maybe the Aztecs want us to find it." Pen blushed when she heard her own words. What was she saying? She didn't believe in this stuff. "I mean—"

"I think you're right. I think the codex wants to be found and we have to find it before Professor Flores does."

Quin handed her a page full of tiny Spanish writing. "Oh, Abuelito," she sighed. The notes blurred as she realized she was holding their only connection to their grandfather and his quest. Had he suspected Professor Flores would double-cross him and leave him in the hospital? She glared down the long aisle at the curtain separating coach and business class. Pen became more determined than ever to crack this mystery.

"Rise and shine," a voice chirped. "We're landing soon and you don't want to miss breakfast."

Quin rubbed his eyes and squinted at Camila. How could she be so perky after such a long flight? Abuelito's notes were still spread across the tray tables. He didn't re-member falling asleep. Pen hunched over her tray table, her arms folded and her head resting on top. A string of drool dribbled out of the corner of her mouth. He toyed with the idea of snapping her picture and sending it to Mi-chael Blalock but decided against it. His sister could hold a grudge a long time.

"Wake up." He poked her a little harder than necessary.

She lashed out with her hand. He ducked, smacking his nose on the tray table and jostling his glasses. "Hey, watch out." He gingerly checked his nose and glasses for damage.

Pen blinked at him sleepily. "Oh, sorry. I was dreaming four Aztec priests were chasing me and they all looked like Professor Flores. They wanted to sacrifice me to the god of fire and acne."

"That sounds terrible." Quin couldn't remember his own dreams, but they'd left him unsettled, too. He decided not to tell her about the red bump starting to form on her chin.

Pen rubbed her face and found the string of drool. Her eyes widened and she swiped at it with a napkin while glaring at him. "Quin, you didn't take any—"

"No." He cut her off. "But speaking of pictures…" He be-gan sorting through the notes. "Where's the Eagle War-rior? You didn't drool on it, did you?"

Pen shuffled through papers and shook her head.

"Where is it?" Quin asked, his voice panicky. Neither twin came up with the painting.

"No. We can't have lost it." He looked under their feet

and even in the empty folder. No painting. No warrior.

"Professor Flores," his twin said. "He must have snuck back here while we were sleeping and taken the painting."

"We would have noticed," he protested, but stopped. She had slept so hard she'd drooled all over herself in public. And he couldn't remember falling asleep, a sure sign he'd been exhausted.

"Some investigators we are," she said. "We lost our only link to the codex."

"Excuse me." The young mother in front of them popped her head over the seat. She had dark circles under her eyes and cast an exasperated glance at her screaming child. She held up a dark piece of paper. "Is this yours? I found one of my children coloring it."

Quin's heart nearly stopped. The Eagle Warrior glared at them indignantly, his face highlighted in purple crayon. He took the paper wordlessly and stared at the painting.

"Thank you," Pen said.

He put the painting back in the folder. She collected the rest of the notes and handed them to him.

"I think the purple gives him more personality."

"This is four-hundred-year-old art," he groaned. He closed the folder and slipped it into his backpack. "It doesn't need more personality."

Professor Flores was waiting for them when they disembarked. "Niños, I trust you had a pleasant flight." He smirked and turned away without waiting for an answer.

Pen glowered at his back. His white shirt was rumpled, and his ponytail drooped. At least he wouldn't look his best when they met their mother. She brightened a little at the thought. Even though she was angry with Mamá for making them travel with the professor, at least she was on her way to meet them. They trailed him through the busy Madrid airport.

"I've been thinking about our investigation," Quin said.

Pen frowned. She didn't like the way this was going.

"When we see Mamá, we should tell her everything. If Professor Flores attacked Abuelito, he's dangerous. We have to tell the police."

"But we won't find the codex then."

"Someone might if we tell the police our story."

She sighed and chewed on her lip. Ahead of them, the professor continued through the airport, seemingly oblivious to whether the twins followed him or not. They could dodge away if they wanted, she realized. Maybe they should hide in the bathroom until he was gone, but they were supposed to meet Mamá. What would she think if they didn't appear?

"Do we have to find it?" Quin asked her. His eyes behind his glasses were serious. "Remember what the last message said? Leave the codex in the past."

Pen sighed and wrestled with conflicting feelings. She wanted to find the codex for Abuelito. And, if she was honest, for herself. She needed to know she could do this. But the investigation felt more dangerous than ever. She felt a rush of gratitude that Quin was still with her. What would she do if anything happened to him? Then she'd be all alone.

"I guess we can tell Mamá," she agreed.

When they reached the baggage carousel, Professor Flores finally acknowledged them.

"Did your grandfather ever discuss what he was researching with you?"

The twins cast each other wary glances.

"Abuelito discusses lots of things with us," Pen said.

The man sighed and gave them an exasperated look. "Bueno, let's talk freely. I understand you are both smart for your age, or at least Maria says so."

Professor Flores made it sound like being twelve was so beneath him he could barely notice their existence.

"I think you know the project I am referring to. The research of a certain painted book."

"What about it?" she asked flatly.

The professor raised his eyebrows. "So you do know of it?"

She bit her lip. She couldn't believe she'd fallen for his trap.

"Only that Abuelito was…is," Quin corrected himself, "interested in Aztec codices. He showed us one at the museum."

Professor Flores waved this information away. "That's it? Nothing else? Nothing you walked across at the bookshop?"

"The expression is 'ran across,'" Pen corrected in her most obnoxious tone. "How did you know we were at the bookshop anyway? Were you following us?"

"Qué ridículo. I have better ways to spend my time than following children."

Pen gave him a skeptical look and gestured to their location. The professor glowered at her. "This is different. This is a favor for your mother."

"Then why were you at the bookshop if you weren't following us?" she asked.

The professor frowned, and she felt a surge of triumph. They were beating him at his own game, or at least staying even.

"Because your grandfather gave me the name of the shop owner as a potential contact in our research."

"Our research? Who are you working with? Someone in a red hat?"

He stared at her as if Pen had lost her mind. "What does a red hat have to…" He shook his head. "Never mind. I'm working with your grandfather, of course."

"You mean you were until you double-crossed Abuelito and hurt him," she shouted.

The baggage carousel screeched and jerked into motion. Suitcases began tumbling through a plastic curtain onto the rotating metal. Travelers shoved past the children to retrieve their bags.

"What are you talking about?" the professor asked impatiently. "I didn't hurt Miguel. I traveled all the way to Mexico to talk to him. Why would I hurt him before we'd even had time to discuss the codex?"

"But why ask us about the codex if you're working with Abuelito? Wouldn't you know more than us?" Quin asked.

Professor Flores ran a hand through his hair, then stared at it. He wiped it on his pants. "We had a disagreement about how to pursue the codex. Your grandfather felt it was

becoming too dangerous. He wouldn't speak to me by phone. I wanted to talk to him in person."

"You were the person Abuelito was yelling at on his cell phone," Pen said, putting it together.

"Your grandfather refused to see me at first." His voice rose and the frazzled mother from the flight looked curiously at them. "But I had to see him. Someone sent me a page recently, a painting I thought might be connected to our search." He shook his head. "I was in Miguel's office when he had a call from the Libreria Madero, when the bookshop owner said he'd received a package for your grandfather."

"Eavesdropper," Pen muttered

Professor Flores advanced toward them. The twins automatically backpedaled, but the baggage carousel cut them off. He stood so close to them she could see the pores of his nose. She leaned back, feeling the luggage shuffle by behind her.

"Your grandfather wasn't hiding anything from me. Why would he? We're partners. We're both searching for the same thing."

"No, you're looking for the codex so you can sell it and make lots of money," Quin accused. "Or maybe so you can add it to your fancy private collection."

The professor's face darkened. "You have no idea why I'm searching for this book. I saw something inside your bag at the security check in Mexico. Give it to me."

"Give you what?" Pen asked. The luggage thunked along the carousel. One suitcase bumped her leg and turned sideways, getting stuck. Other luggage began to build up behind it.

"My page from the Codex Cardona. I don't know how you got it, but it came to me. It was stolen off my desk."

She glanced around wildly. The baggage terminal was packed with people from several international flights. It would be hard to rush past the man. The luggage continued to back up as one suitcase slammed into another. "We don't know what you're talking about," her brother said. His voice quavered.

The professor's lips tightened until they went white. "The flight attendant informed me you two were studying quite hard on the flight." He shook his head. "On summer break? What were you reading? Did Miguel happen to give you his notes? I couldn't find them in his office or at his house." He reached out and grabbed Quin's backpack.

"Quin," Pen shrieked. She wrestled the jammed suitcase off the carousel. The backed-up luggage flooded forward, scattering suitcases everywhere. The professor lunged at them but stumbled over a hard-shelled case and fell to the floor. She leaped onto the carousel and Quin followed.

They ran down the moving circle, their feet pounding the metal panels. Soon, they reached another section full of luggage. Pen didn't hesitate. She used the luggage as stepping stones. The bags shifted beneath her, knocking her off balance. She stumbled and banged her knee. She pushed up and glanced back to check on Quin, but she'd reached the end of the carousel and the luggage was turning the corner. Her foot lodged between two heavy suitcases and the momentum of the carousel pushed her forward. As the baggage swung around the corner, she toppled off the carousel.

Pen fell hard onto the tile floor. One of the suitcases tumbled after her and crashed onto her legs. She heard the shocked murmurs of people around her, but she focused on her brother. He was still on the carousel, trying to maneuver through the luggage, but the motion worked against him like a hamster desperately in danger of falling off its wheel.

He gripped his backpack with one hand and his glasses with the other. Behind him, Professor Flores used his tall frame to shove people out of the way, and most had stopped retrieving their luggage anyway while they watched Quin struggle to stay on top of the carousel. The professor angled closer and Pen realized they would reach the end of the carousel at the same time.

She shoved the luggage off her and tried to stand, only to find the world spinning as if she were still with her twin on the carousel. "Watch out," she called.

Quin dove to the top of the carousel, but the professor caught the heel of his sneaker, cutting his leap short. He fell onto a suitcase. The professor jerked him off the carousel and he tumbled onto the floor. Pen dashed to him, ready to defend her brother.

"The painting," Professor Flores snarled. He reached down and grasped Quin's t-shirt, using his free hand to grab the backpack. "Where is it?"

Quin yelped and twisted away. With one strap still looped over his arm, he tried to pull the backpack free. Pen clawed at the hand holding the t-shirt, but the professor didn't release him. She stamped hard on his foot.

Professor Flores howled and let loose a string of Spanish words La Condesa would never approve of, but he didn't let go of Quin or the backpack. She despaired. If the professor took the notes, they'd never find the codex. They wouldn't know who'd attacked Abuelito. They couldn't help him. Tears stung her eyes. She took a deep breath, filling her lungs with air for her last resort—screaming like a girl.

Thwack! A long metallic object cracked across Professor Flores' arm. The professor let go of Quin with a high-pitched shriek, much to Pen's satisfaction. He flew into a stream of Spanish curse words, but this tirade was cut short when the metal stick whacked him on the head.

"Not another word," a familiar voice thundered. "Let go of these children."

She stepped around Professor Flores for a better look and her brother scrambled up. Their rescuer held one silver crutch out like a sword and leaned heavily on the other. His face was as purple as the Eagle Warrior—if you disregarded the bushy white hair and beard.

"Kostas," the twins shouted at the same time. The Greek professor glanced over at them and gave a small nod. "My Gemini twins. What is the meaning of this?"

18

Airport security surrounded them. Quin surveyed the serious men in uniforms with the even more serious guns in their hands and shuffled closer to Kostas, glad the Greek tutor had such a wide girth. He was still out of breath from the chase on the baggage conveyer belt. Professor Flores immediately began speaking to the policía in rapid fire Spanish. Quin frowned and tried to focus on the words, but Professor Flores' Spanish accent threw him off. He caught enough to realize the professor claimed the twins had stolen something of his.

Kostas let the professor rattle on and balanced on his crutches. He turned to each twin and asked, "Are you well?"

They both nodded. Pen pointed to Professor Flores. "He thinks we—"

"Wait," Kostas said. "Tempus omnia revelat."

She groaned. "Kostas, you're not going to—"

"Translation?"

"Time reveals all things," Quin said.

"Correct. And who said this?"

"You did," Pen muttered. Kostas glanced back at her. His brown eyes glowed beneath his unkempt eyebrows. The same unruly hair covered his chin and lips and even poked from his nose. His wink was almost hidden in the deep sun creases of his brown skin. Quin couldn't help but smile. Kostas was with them. Everything would be okay.

His sister sighed. "Aeschylus, I think."

"Good." Kostas turned back to the animated conversation between the professor and the policía. Quin raised his eyebrows at her, impressed. She stuck out her tongue.

"And these children stole it from me."

The professor's words caught their attention. "No es cierto. That's not true," Quin protested.

"We didn't take anything from him," Pen added.

The police captain rubbed his forefinger between his eyebrows and muttered to his men to get back to work. They shooed away the huge crowd gathered around them.

"Come with me," he told the children, Kostas, and Professor Flores. "We'll finish this in my office."

The police captain's cramped office smelled of dirty laundry and cigarettes. Confiscated suitcases piled on top of each other like a broken carousel. Professor Flores immediately took the only chair, leaving Kostas leaning on his crutches.

"Check the boy's backpack," the professor said. "You'll find the stolen piece of art. It's extremely valuable."

Quin shook his head vigorously and wished he could say a few magic words to make the Eagle Warrior become invisible.

The captain turned to the twins and Kostas and sighed. "Searching the backpack would be the quickest way to solve this accusation."

"I'm not a thief," Quin shouted. He considered dashing out of the office, but another policeman stood at the door.

"He's the liar." Pen pointed to Professor Flores. "He said our mother would be waiting for us in Spain."

The police captain's expression shifted from doubt to alarm. "Your mother? What do you mean by this? Did this man kidnap you?"

At the word kidnap, Professor Flores froze, and his dark eyes grew large. He opened his mouth but couldn't seem to find the right words. "Kidnap? No. Their grandfather—I'm a family friend— Maria said—"

The police captain looked back at her, his face grave. "You must tell the truth. Were you kidnapped?"

Quin could see the struggle on her face. If the police thought Professor Flores was a kidnapper, they'd have the freedom they needed to track down the Codex Cardona themselves. And it served him right for attacking them and trying to take the Eagle Warrior. But calling him a kidnapper was serious, and they hadn't been entirely honest with their grandparents about the codex, either. He shook his head at Pen. She nodded slowly.

"No," Pen told the police captain. "He was accompanying us to Spain, and we were supposed to meet my mother here." She stopped. "Wait, where is Mamá?"

In all the confusion, Quin had momentarily forgotten his mother was supposed to meet them, not Kostas.

The Greek professor's wrinkled face softened, and he pursed his lips. "My deepest pardon, children. I was unable to deliver the message from your mother because this man was attacking you when I arrived." He gave Professor Flores a stern look and the police captain added his own.

"Your mother," he continued, "was able to get an unexpected flight off the island and decided to go to Mexico City immediately."

The twins shared a look. If Mamá had gone straight to Mexico, things with Abuelito couldn't be good. Quin gripped his backpack and tried to find his voice. It took several tries to speak, and it came out as a whisper.

"Is everything okay?" He could hardly get the next words out. "Is Abuelito...is he—"

"Your grandfather is the same. Which is to say, not better, but not worse. He simply is and what will be remains to be seen."

He was afraid their tutor would quote another dead philosopher, but he merely pressed his lips together until they disappeared beneath his mustache and beard.

"Of course," Pen said, her voice bitter. "She strands us in Spain after sending us here in the first place." She kicked a discarded suitcase. Quin tried to catch her eyes to let his sister know he shared her dismay, but she'd turned away.

"Your father is flying here tomorrow morning," Kostas said. "I was able to get away the quickest, which is why I'm here to meet you. We will see what Maria thinks about your grandfather. It may be one or both of your parents will have to cancel their summer plans."

"Perdón," the police captain said. "I am sorry to hear of the children's predicament, but I must clear up this misunderstanding. It is indeed a misunderstanding, isn't it?"

His eyes flicked to his desk hidden beneath several thick files of paperwork.

"But the painting," Professor Flores protested. "I am willing to let this unseemly incident go if I can have it."

"You're the one who attacked us." Pen glowered at him.

The police captain sighed and reached out to Quin. "I'm sorry. This is the simplest way." He tugged at the backpack and, after a moment, Quin released it, his heart sinking. The police captain unzipped the backpack and rummaged around. The twins stared at each other, their thoughts the same. Professor Flores would see the Eagle Warrior and Abuelito's notes too. He would know exactly what they were up to and their investigation would be over.

The man slid out the file folder holding the Eagle Warrior. Quin held his breath and stared at the floor, feeling as if he'd betrayed the warrior. He should have fought harder to keep him safe, just like he should have supported Pen when she protested against traveling to Spain with Professor Flores. And if he'd told Abuelito about their investigation, maybe their grandfather wouldn't be in the hospital right now. How many people would he let down?

"Is this what you're looking for?" the police captain asked. He dangled the paper in front of Professor Flores. "This is nothing but a child's drawing."

Professor Flores' eyes widened at the purple scribble

around the Eagle Warrior's head. Contrasted with the other bright colors on the page and the bent edges where the folder had failed to protect the painting, it did indeed look less noble and more like a child's invention.

The professor gasped and turned to Quin. "How dare you—"

"My brother's an artist," Pen piped up. She turned to the police captain and reached for the painting. "Isn't it good?" She lifted her eyebrows and tilted her head slightly. "Except I don't know what he was thinking about this purple scribbling."

"It's unique," the captain agreed. "Especially the head." He glanced at the pile of notes in the folder.

"That's just homework," Quin said. "Kostas always assigns us a research project over the summer."

He held his breath and glanced at their friend. The Greek pursed his lips, looking like a stern Santa who had placed him on the naughty list. "It is true I assign them a project each summer."

The police captain slipped the painting over the notes and closed the folder. He handed it and the backpack back. "I think everything is in order here."

Professor Flores stood up. "But the painting is mine. I found it first. Someone took it from me and then this boy ruined it."

The police captain fixed him with a stern look. "Aren't you too old to be playing games with these children? Their behavior I can excuse but yours..." He shook his head and spoke to Kostas over the children's heads. "You're free to go. Please keep those crutches to yourself." He nodded goodbye to the children.

"Are you going to arrest—" Pen started to ask, but Kostas grabbed her shoulder and pushed them both from the room, maneuvering them and managing his crutches at the same time.

"Don't look a gift horse in the mouth."

"Are we supposed to tell you who said that?" Quin

couldn't resist asking, even as he hurried them away from security.

"No," he said. "Besides, nobody knows the original author of that particular idiom. Let's get your luggage and leave before Professor Flores is released."

He stopped and grasped the arms of both children. "And then," Kostas announced, giving them his no-nonsense look, "you'll explain to me why you're carrying such an ancient and slightly desecrated piece of Mexican art inside Quin's backpack and why you lied to the police about it."

A yellow-striped umbrella shaded their table at the edge of the Plaza Mayor. Tourists and pigeons milled about Madrid's oldest city square. Kostas ordered a late-morning café and the twins sipped orange soda from round bottles. Quin drank his slowly between bites of the olives, bread, and meatballs the Greek professor had ordered as snacks. It wasn't quite lunch time. Now that they were away from the airport and Professor Flores, he felt more anxious about the entire incident. He didn't know if Pen saw the crazed look in the professor's eye when he shouted for the children to give him the painting. His backpack sat between his feet, one strap looped around his leg to discourage pickpockets. He sucked on an olive, twisted his mouth at the bitter taste, and washed it down with sweet soda.

Kostas explained how their mother was able to catch a flight with a doctor who'd been suddenly called to the mainland. Getting a flight to Mexico City from there had been easy.

"Maria would have called you," he said, "but you were already in the air. So she asked me to come instead. She couldn't locate your father. I believe he was in the middle of an experiment at CERN."

"You said Abuelito was the same," Quin said. "Is he or not?"

Kostas licked olive juice off his fingers and wiped them on his beard. He stared off at the center of the square until he thought he might not answer, but he swung his gaze back to the children and squinted. "What I said is true. Your grandfather is the same."

He paused. Quin had finished his soda and was rolling the bottle between his palms. He tipped it over accidentally and it clinked on the table. He put his hands in his lap. "But it is worse," he said quietly, "because Abuelito hasn't woken up yet." He looked up to find his tutor's gentle eyes on him. Kostas nodded once.

"That is correct, Quintus. A good deduction, though regrettable subject matter."

Despite the hot sun beating down on their umbrella and the heat radiating up from the cobblestones, a chill rushed through him. How much longer would Abuelito sleep? Forever?

"Now..." Their friend swigged the last of his coffee. "Let's see this ancient artwork again."

Quin removed the Eagle Warrior from his bag and Pen shoved the empty dishes out of the way so they could spread the painting across the table. Kostas studied it silently for several minutes, his eyes moving so slowly across the page Quin had to look twice to see they moved at all. The man was first and foremost an archeologist, like their mother, and Maria Grey Reyes had acquired her eye for detail under his tutelage. Finally, Kostas sat back and sighed, rubbing a large hand across his bushy beard. A few bread crumbs trickled onto his belly. He dusted them to the ground and bemusedly watched a few sparrows battle for the treat.

"I see Miguel has involved you in his search. Perhaps a wise decision, perhaps not. Time, as you know, will tell."

"You mean you know about the Codex Cardona?" Quin smoothed his hand across the warrior's face, feeling the oiliness in the purple crayon markings. Guilt crept through him and he averted his eyes from the warrior's stony stare.

"Of course I do."

"For a huge secret, a whole lot of people seem to know about it," Pen said.

The man laughed, a sound both twins loved. It started deep in his belly and by the time it reached his mouth, it resonated like a baritone.

"You must not forget I've known your family a long time. Maria told me about her father's search. She even helped your grandfather one summer when she was home from her field studies."

"She did?" both twins cried.

"Abuelito never told us," Pen said.

Kostas shook his head. "The last I heard, the trail had gone cold and your grandfather had lost a friend who was searching with him."

Lost?" Quin asked. "You mean…" He gulped, a meatball sticking in his throat. "You mean dead?"

The tutor shrugged. "He disappeared several years ago and with him, any connections Miguel had to the Codex Cardona. Your mother and grandmother asked him to stop the search. I believed he'd given up on ever finding the codex." He gave them a measured look. "At least, until this summer."

The twins exchanged a look over their empty bottles. First, their grandfather's friend disappeared, then Abuelito was attacked.

"Abuelito said some people thought the painted book was cursed," Quin said slowly. The thought made the food in his stomach turn over. Could it be cursed? Was that why their grandfather was hurt?

Kostas nodded and gazed at the Eagle Warrior. "I have found many artifacts in my studies, but I've learned you cannot find them until they want to be found." He handed the warrior back to Quin, who put the painting back into the file folder and closed it, suddenly finding the eyes too accusing.

"Don't be stupid," Pen snapped. "Curses are

superstitions people make up when they lack scientific evidence for the truth."

"I'm not stupid." He glared across the table at her.

"You are if you actually believe that stuff."

"Gemeni," Kostas said, using the familiar nickname for them. He placed a large hand firmly on each of their shoulders. "Familia est omnia. Translation?"

"Family is everything," she said through gritted teeth. The look on her face told Quin she didn't believe it, and there they were, half a world away from all their family, except for each other. Perhaps she had the same thought. She sighed. "Sorry, Quin, you're not stupid."

He nodded, then flashed her a quick grin. "I know I'm not, but it's good to be reminded."

"Bene." Kostas used the Latin word for good. "As it turns out, you're both correct about the curse."

"You mean you believe in curses?" Pen asked, incredulous. "But you're a scientist."

He laughed again, and the twins couldn't help smiling with him. "I am, and deeply committed to the truth based on evidence. However," he tapped his nose, "sometimes what people believe is closer to the truth than what science can tell us."

She scrunched up her nose and blew a stray strand of hair away from her face. Pen often did this while she thought something over. At least she was considering it, Quin thought. He polished his glasses on his t-shirt, as if this would help him see the truth more clearly. Why did Kostas have to speak in riddles?

He pushed his glasses back on his nose. "You mean it doesn't matter if there's a curse or not? If people believe there is, things will happen that make it seem like it's true?"

"Or if people believe there is a curse, then they behave that way and set off a chain of events that make it appear the curse has come true," his sister added.

Kostas smiled at them. "Exactly." He gestured to the

waiter for the check. "Now, about finding that codex."

Quin caught his breath. He'd expected their investigation to be over.

"You mean you'll help us look for it?" Pen asked.

"Even with the curse?" Quin asked. "Or mysterious chain of events," he hurried to add, seeing the frown on his twin's face.

Kostas shrugged his broad shoulders. "If there is a curse, or events have been set in motion, then you two are already part of them. It's my duty to make sure you're protected."

"You want to know where the codex is," Quin said, not fooled. "You can't resist finding an ancient artifact."

The tutor might have been smiling beneath his beard. "That, too, Gemini." He chuckled. "That, too."

19

Kostas suggested they begin their search at the Museo de América, which actually housed other codices. They took the metro across town, packed tightly into the train car as people headed to lunch.

Pen wrinkled her nose at the smell of so many warm bodies squished together. At least with so many people in the car, they could get lost in the crowd more easily. The fight with Professor Flores had rattled her more than she would admit. She wondered where he was and if he'd follow them now that he knew for certain they had the Eagle Warrior.

The metro's audio system calmly informed them they were nearing the next stop. Kostas studied the map on the metro wall. She studied the one on her smartphone. "This is us."

He shook his head. "Soon, you won't need teachers at all. Just these devices. I will be obsolete."

"We'll always need you," Quin said. Pen nodded. She wouldn't have said it out loud, but she was glad to have Kostas with them. Being an international investigator was more dangerous than she'd thought.

The Museo de América bore more of a resemblance to a cathedral than a museum. It had a tall bell tower on one end of the building and a grand entry with a wide staircase leading to double doors of arched glass. The red brick building reminded her of St. Mary's, her school in Boston. She wondered what Michael Blalock was doing right now. Probably playing soccer with another girl at soccer camp and having a fine time of it. Maybe she should text him.

Her phone dinged like it had a mind of its own. Nearly, she thought. She had a fleeting hope it was Michael, but of course, it was Archie. She smiled as she read the words before they could fade. She checked his location and was surprised to see he wasn't on campus but in Boston instead.

α: Safe arrival in Spain, I see. On another field trip?

π: Investigating.

α: Oh? What r u investigating?

Pen hesitated. She hated keeping things from her brother, but they were back on the trail of the codex and she couldn't risk anyone else getting hurt. Not until they solved the mystery.

π: It's a secret. Don't worry. Kostas is here.

Archie's signature α floated on the map, well away from MIT.

π: You on a field trip 2?

His answer didn't come immediately.

α: 2 can keep secrets. Stay out of trouble.

"Wake up," Quin said. Pen had zombie-walked up the staircase and into Kostas' back while she texted. She said goodbye to Archie and tucked the phone away, not quite stifling a yawn.

"We need to be alert," her brother said. "We might find something here to tell us where the codex is, and we don't have a lot of time."

"Before it closes?" She fought off another yawn. The all-night flight was catching up with her. And what could Archie be keeping secret from her?

Quin shook his head. "No, before Dad meets us tomorrow and we lose our chance to find the codex for Abuelito forever."

"Oh, yeah. That." She pushed Archie out of her mind. She had enough to focus on right now.

Kostas had been holding an in-depth discussion with a museum guide. Their voices rose until they were nearly shouting. Apparently, Greeks and Spaniards bargained the same way—noisily. If they were trying to be discreet, they weren't now.

Kostas waved the children over. "Alfonso is going to give us a tour of the museum. I've told him we're only interested in seeing the painted books for your school project."

The guide looked only slightly older than Archie. He motioned them into the building. Pen noticed immediately the museum was laid out almost the same as Abuelito's—a square of four connected hallways with a large open courtyard in the middle. Alfonso took them to a dark room with thick panels of glass crisscrossing the room. Behind the panels were rows of drawings in bright colors, some with black writing down the side, others without.

"Wow." Quin walked to the wall of glass and began browsing the paintings slowly. Pen trailed him.

"There's one like our warrior," she cried, pointing to a similarly dressed soldier wearing brightly painted armor and holding a shield. "Without the purple head." He shot her a dark look.

Alfonso began a memorized spiel about the history of the codex Tudela, the one on display before them. Pen only half listened as he told them how it represented Aztec religion and culture as it had been around the 1550s, a good thirty years after the conquistadors arrived in Mexico. Then, one comment caught her attention.

"Did you say this codex was found in the 1940s?"

The guide paused. "Comó?" he responded in Spanish, then switched back to English, much to her relief. "Yes, 1940 exactly."

"Where was it before that?"

He shrugged. "Quíen sabe? These things sometimes

appear after long periods of time. Usually, they've been held illegally, but museums are willing to overlook this and pay millions to own a piece as valuable as this codex. Private collectors, too."

Quin poked Pen and mouthed, "Like Professor Flores."

They all gazed at the codex. Lights shone from the ceiling, illuminating the painted figures frozen for all time. Priests dressed in brilliant headdresses of quetzal feathers wielded sharp knives and performed human sacrifices. Blood ran down their arms and stained their priestly garments. She shivered as she studied them, the idea of cutting out human hearts chilling even now.

Other pages were not so frightening. Men and women worked in the fields. Women also cooked over fires and Pen thought of Camila. She felt a pang of loss and wondered where the tortilla maker painting was now. Had Professor Flores stolen it from Abuelito's office, as she suspected?

"A fine presentation," Kostas said, and she realized Alfonso had stopped speaking. "Did you hear, children? He asked if you had any questions."

Their tutor waited expectantly, as if there was indeed a question they should be asking. They looked at each other, mystified. "Let's see," Pen said, loud enough for Quin's ears only. "This codex came to the museum in 1940. It was hidden before that. Lost. Like Abuelito's friend."

"Disappeared from history," her brother said. He straightened his glasses and stared at the drawings. "We're missing something important."

"If this codex was hidden for so long," Pen continued, "and then discovered, isn't it possible…" She didn't finish her sentence. She knew he would understand. If the codex Tudela had been discovered, why couldn't the Codex Cardona turn up in the same way, found mysteriously after all these years?

But who could have hidden it away? And who was sending out pages now to Abuelito and Professor Flores?

"Alfonso." Quin turned suddenly. The guide had his hand out to Kostas, who placed a few coins in it.

"Sí?" He closed his hand over the money and tucked it into his pocket.

"Who bought this codex for the museum?"

He checked his watch and shrugged. "The director, I suppose. I haven't studied that."

"Could we talk to him?" Pen asked, catching onto her twin's train of thought.

The guide shook his head. "He retired several years ago. Would you like a tour of anything else today? There's an exquisite display of New World gold from Colombia."

"No, thank you," Kostas said. "We only have time for the one tour. Children, don't we have somewhere else to be?"

"Yes," Quin said. Pen nodded her agreement.

The tutor beamed at them. "Bene. Make haste slowly."

"Augustus Caesar," they chimed at the same time.

At the museum's customer service desk, a woman with long dark hair and bright red lips looked up from her computer and squinted at them. "Necesitan asistencia?" Assistance sounded like the last thing she wanted to offer.

"Can you tell us who the museum director was until a few years ago?" Quin asked.

The woman frowned. "That's an unusual request. I've only been here a year." She typed into the computer. "Do you have a complaint you wish to notify our current director about? The museum is not to your liking?"

"It's wonderful," Pen said.

He turned to look at his twin. Usually, he had to drag her to museums. Maybe being an international investigator was a good thing after all.

"We'd just like to talk to the retired director about..." She paused.

"About one of the pieces he acquired," he finished. "It's for a school project."

The woman nodded vaguely and typed. "Here it is. An article on the director's sudden retirement. His name is Francisco Rivera."

The twins gasped at the same time and stared at each other. "But isn't that the name of Abuelito's friend?" she said. "The one who disappeared?"

He nodded, certain of it, and turned to Kostas. "Did you know Abuelito's friend was the director here?"

He put a hand to his lips and shrugged. Quin understood he didn't want to talk here. Maybe their tutor would make a good international agent, too.

"Let's find a hotel," the man suggested. "Then we can discuss this more."

"Oh, let's." Pen ran a hand through her hair. He examined his rumpled shirt. A hotel did sound nice. He felt exhausted from the long plane ride. Even international agents had to take breaks sometimes.

"Gracias," he told the woman at the desk. She barely nodded as they hurried away.

Traveling with Kostas made things easier. Adults like to question twelve-year-olds who are on their own, but with their Greek companion, they never gave a second glance unless it was at the professor's wild hair and beard. He checked them into two adjacent rooms in a quaint two-story hotel. Its low-hanging wrought iron balconies and clay pots full of blooming red and gold geraniums reminded Pen of a picture from a travel account.

As soon as they entered their room, she pulled her laptop out and connected to the internet, searching for anything about Francisco Rivera. She scrolled through the results and blew hair out of her eyes.

"Too many hits. Here's one on a bullfighter. And a movie star. And a boxer." She scanned through the first page, then the second. "We'll never find him this way."

Her brother turned to Kostas, who sat in an armchair

near the balcony, silent as usual.

"If you knew about Abuelito's friend, why didn't you say anything?"

The man tapped a finger on his knee. Seconds passed, and Pen sighed, wishing she could hurry the old man into answering. But she'd learned there was no hurrying him.

"I didn't know you were looking for Francisco," Kostas finally said.

"But you knew he disappeared and Abuelito was looking for him?" She frowned at the screen and chose another search engine. Sometimes, you had to work the system.

Their companion cleared his throat gently. "I knew your grandfather searched for Francisco when he first disappeared several years ago. He gave up the search abruptly, saying it was at your grandmother's request. I always suspected something else made him stop."

"The curse?" Quin suggested.

Pen rolled her eyes. "Not that again. More like someone."

"So Abuelito didn't start looking again until Professor Flores contacted him," her brother said. "And then he got attacked. Sounds like the curse to me."

Kostas closed his eyes and rubbed at the leg in the cast. She had nearly forgotten their tutor might be in pain. "How's your leg?" she asked.

He grimaced. "I won't return to any digs for a while."

She shot him a sympathetic glance, then hunched over her laptop and muttered to herself.

Quin pulled out Abuelito's notes and shuffled through them.

"What are you looking for?" she whispered. She couldn't tell if the tutor was asleep or not.

Her brother frowned. "I don't know exactly. Something feels off about Abuelito's friend." Kostas started snoring softly. Pen tapped at her keyboard and kept one eye on her brother. He pulled out a note and showed it to her. It was one of the earliest entries they had.

2 de febrero, 1966

Francisco returned to Spain like a conquistador to take an internship with the Museo de America in Madrid. I will miss our aventuras together, but lately, he was becoming obsessed with our search for the Codex Cardona. It is as if he is Don Quijote and I am his Sancho, always holding him to reality when all he wants is to live in a past that cannot be recouped.

He has even taken to calling himself Bernardino, after the great monk Bernardino de Sahagún, and insists I refer to him this way in all matters of the Codex Cardona. When I protest, he quotes Quixote himself, saying "I know who I am and who I may be, if I choose."

Perhaps separation is what we both need, and now I can focus on my own research and of course, la Bella Inez, whom I intend to marry with all haste.

"Francisco," her brother shouted. "It's him."

Kostas jerked awake and rubbed the ear closest to Quin. "Where is the fire, Gemini?"

Pen jumped up and took another look at the note. "What do you mean?"

He pointed triumphantly to a name and read the letter aloud. She sat beside him on the bed in a moment of rare patience. She felt rather tired, actually, and didn't push him to get to his point like she normally would.

"In his notes, Abuelito always talks about Bernardino," he said. "We thought he meant Bernardino de Sahagún, the monk who lived with the Aztecs. But he didn't. He meant his friend, Francisco Rivera."

"Increíble. So Bernardino is Francisco Rivera? The friend who disappeared?"

Quin nodded. "The only person who might know where the Codex Cardona is."

"You think that's why he disappeared?"

He shrugged. "We know someone else is looking for the

painted book. Maybe they got to Francisco."

"You mean he's dead?" Her voice rose a little. Pen swallowed and took a deep breath, but a shudder ran through her. She didn't want their search to turn into a murder investigation.

Quin frowned and looked at Kostas, but the Greek tutor didn't add his opinion. He often let the twins work through problems on their own. "You said you couldn't find any more information on him, didn't you?"

She nodded. "I only searched under his name, though. I wonder—" She didn't finish but hurried to the computer and typed rapidly. Then, she groaned. Dozens of references peppered the results, almost all of them on Bernardino de Sahagún.

Her brother sighed. "It'll take too long to look at all those pages. We'll never find him, if he's still alive."

"Maybe," she said. "I have an idea." Her fingers flew over the keys.

"What are you doing?" her twin asked. He leaned over her shoulder. Normally, this annoyed her, but she chose to ignore it.

"A trick Archie taught me to narrow the search parameters. I'm replacing the default code with my own." She punched the return key hard and held her breath. The search screen flashed up and she gasped. The search returned one result and it was so unexpected neither twin spoke.

Kostas stirred from his chair. He grabbed a crutch and limped over to the desk.

Quin found his voice. "So he's alive?"

"Technology doesn't lie." She pointed to the words on the screen. The website was a listing of monks currently living in monasteries in Spain and the search had highlighted one name—Fray Bernardino Rivera—El monasterio de San Lorenzo.

"San Lorenzo?" the tutor said. "It is not far from Madrid. And it is not only a monastery but a former palace.

Beneath its basilica are the tombs of many Spanish kings."
He put a hand on their shoulders. "Think of the history we
could see."

"Can we go?" Pen asked.

He tugged on one ear and shook his head. "We are to
meet your father tomorrow morning. Perhaps afterward,
if there is time, we can go but…" He frowned. "I admit, I'm
reluctant, my Gemeni. This disagreement with Professor
Flores, your grandfather's attack…it is unsettling."

"But Kostas, we're so close to finding Abuelito's friend,
and maybe the codex, too. We have to go." She resisted
stamping her foot with this statement.

"But if Kostas isn't sure," her brother said.

"Come on, Quin," Pen whispered. "Don't you want to finish the investigation?"

He nodded. "Pen's right. We have to go. For Abuelito."

"For Abuelito," she echoed.

Kostas sighed and shook his head. "I am sorry, but my
responsibility is to your parents. We stay here until your
father arrives."

When she opened her mouth to argue, he raised one
massive hand to quiet her. "There is an appointed time for
everything." He raised his bushy brows and waited.

Both twins shook their heads. Kostas smiled slightly.
"King Solomon. And perhaps this is not the time to find the
Codex Cardona."

A low growl like a lion's warning filled the room. The
Greek professor patted his broad stomach sheepishly.
"Let's all clean up and have a good meal. Everything will
look better in the morning."

Kostas went to his room next door. Pen leaned against
the hotel door, her eyes on the Eagle Warrior. Quin followed her gaze and they both stared at the only piece of
the codex they had. It held the promise of so much more.
The warrior stood tall and regal against the pillow, as if
ready for anything.

"We can't wait," she whispered. "If we do, we'll never

solve the mystery. Dad will take us back to Mexico, or Switzerland, or wherever. He won't care about the codex."

"But what about the curse?" her twin whispered.

She shook her head. "Curse or no curse, we have to find Bernardino now or we'll never have the chance again. The codex may always be lost."

He picked up the Aztec Warrior and nodded. "Looks like we're about to bring two worlds back together again."

20

They ate in the hotel restaurant, which consisted of two tables outside the tiny kitchen at the back of the lobby. Since most Spaniards ate dinner late in the evening, the woman doubling as the receptionist and cook warmed up lunch leftovers.

Quin tore into the potatoes covered in spicy tomato sauce and the creamy custard that followed. Airplane food had left a hole in his stomach, but when he finished, he still felt a little hollow. The knowledge that they were going against Kostas' decision to wait for their father made him queasy.

He returned them to their room, asked them to call their mother, and bid them good night. Pen dialed Mamá from her laptop. Abuelito was the same and the policia had no news on his attacker. Until he woke up, they wouldn't know what had happened. Quin heard the tension in her voice. She barely asked about their flight and if Kostas had met them at the airport and also didn't apologize for the change in plans. They didn't tell her about Professor Flores' attack. She had enough to worry about.

After they said goodbye, Pen pulled up a train schedule. "Look." She pointed to the timetable. "We can catch a train to San Lorenzo until midnight."

"Midnight?" he gasped. He tried not to think of all the

things that could go wrong with this plan. He straightened his glasses and nodded. "Maybe we should wait a little, so Kostas thinks we're asleep."

"Good thinking," she agreed. They packed Abuelito's notes and the Eagle Warrior in his backpack. He paused before tucking the warrior into the bag and studied the proud eyes.

"I think he's as excited as we are," he said, risking a chance that she felt the same about the warrior.

Instead of laughing, she nodded slowly. "I think he wants us to find the codex."

He grinned, glad he wasn't the only one thinking old paintings were talking to him. Her phone dinged, and she grabbed it from the desk. "Archie."

Quin tugged his phone out of his backpack to follow the conversation.

α: Got any more field trips planned?

He caught his breath. How did Archie always know when they were up to something?

π: Do you?

α: Spies never tell. You two ok?

They were about to sneak out and catch a train to a monastery in the middle of the night. Was that doing okay?

K: We're fine. Sleepy. Buenas noches.

Quin texted quickly before he could change his mind.

α: He speaks! If K says everything is ok, I believe it. Buenas noches.

"Nice job." Pen must have read the guilt he felt on his face. She added, "Good investigators sometimes have to keep secrets."

She turned off the light and they both settled down to wait. He stretched out on one of the twin beds and she took the armchair near the window.

"Stay awake," Quin told himself, but jet lag had finally caught up with him. He closed his eyes, wanting to rest them a moment while he thought through this plan to get to San Lorenzo.

A loud banging jarred him from a dreamless sleep. He sat up, his heart hammering, and strained his ears. "What was that?" he asked.

He checked the time. It was after ten. They should already be gone. "We're late."

"Kostas," a voice shouted in the hotel hallway. "Open this door, you swarthy Greek, or I'll wake the entire floor."

"That sounds like—"

"Professor Flores." Quin rubbed his arm where the professor had gripped it that morning.

"How did he find us?" she whispered. She crept silently to the door and pressed her ear to it. He almost followed, but he could hear well enough from the bed. The professor pounded again on the door next to theirs.

Kostas' voice rumbled like thunder warning of a coming storm. "You shouldn't be here after you attacked those children today. I will call the policía if you don't leave now."

Quin couldn't see the Greek, but he imagined the man brandishing his crutches as he had that morning.

"I must speak with you," Professor Flores said. "It's urgent. It's about the Codex Cardona. If you continue to pursue it, you'll be in danger. You may already be. The children, too."

"From you maybe," Kostas shot back. "How do I know you're not here to knock me out and steal the page you claimed the children had this morning?"

"You can't pull one past Kostas," Pen whispered.

"Lo siento," Professor Flores apologized. "I am ashamed of the way I acted. I thought—" He paused, and Quin imagined he was running a hand through his greasy hair. "I thought if I could get the painting, I know the children are carrying, they would lose interest. They must give this up. I thought their mother would meet them and that would be the end of it."

"What is it you are trying so hard not to say?" Kostas had lowered his voice, so the twins barely heard the question.

"I think whoever attacked Miguel Reyes is in Spain. And I think they're after the codex."

In the light from the streetlamp, the twins stared at each other, openmouthed.

"But he's the one who attacked Abuelito," he whispered. "He has the giant head."

Kostas had said nothing. Quin tried to picture the old man's face, creased with sun and age, deliberating over Professor Flores' words the same way he studied ancient artifacts. The floorboards next door creaked loudly as the tutor stepped back. "Come in." The door clicked shut. The twins could hear muffled voices next door, but nothing else.

"Kostas can't believe him," he said. "Who else could have attacked Abuelito? It has to be Professor Flores."

Pen stared at their window. Light from a street lamp shone through the thin curtains of their second-floor room and laughter and music floated up from the street below. Most people in Madrid were just going out for the evening.

"Shouldn't we tell Kostas?"

"Kostas will be fine as long as he's got those crutches," she whispered. "It's us I'm worried about."

"Why?" he asked. He dreaded the answer.

"Because what if Professor Flores convinces Kostas he's right? He'll never let us out of his sight."

He breathed in sharply. "And we'll never get to the monastery to find out if Abuelito's friend is there."

"Or if he knows anything more about the Codex Cardona," she finished.

Next door, the higher-pitched murmur of Professor Flores continued, uninterrupted by Kostas' lower voice.

"We have to go," he said. His sister flashed him a smile.

"I thought you'd never say it."

Second-story windows in Spain weren't nearly as high as

at home, but as Quin peered over the balcony, he thought they were still far too high above the ground. He swung one leg over the wrought iron balcony, trying not to knock off any potted geraniums. "Are you sure we're doing the right thing?" he asked while he still had one foot on solid ground.

Pen brought a finger to her lips and glanced at the window next door. Shadowy figures moved behind the curtains. "It's our last chance."

Quin nodded. He swung his other leg over and then worked his hands down the iron railing until he was squatting. *You can do this,* he told himself. *You've saved penalty kicks before. Leaping in the air is harder than this.* He swallowed and dangled one foot off the edge, then the other. Quin hung for a second, feeling the iron bars dig into his fingers and trying not to look down.

"Let go," his sister whispered. "Before anyone sees you."

He shut his eyes and let go. His feet hit the ground almost immediately, and he bent quickly at the knees, absorbing the impact. He put one hand on the sidewalk for balance and took a deep breath. Amazing. He couldn't believe he hadn't hurt himself.

"Move," Pen whispered above him. Her feet dangled in his face. The drop wasn't nearly as far as he'd thought. He felt a little sheepish and scooted over as she dropped to the ground next to him.

He glanced around, but no one had noticed two kids falling from the sky. The balconies opened onto a side street and anyone walking by was probably not looking down the alley.

"Let's go," she said. "We have to get to the train station before it closes."

They jogged down the alleyway and onto the main road, blinded momentarily by the bright lights of bars and cafés still packed with customers.

"Thank goodness nobody goes to bed early here," Pen

said.

"When in Rome," Quin whispered. It was one of Kostas' favorite expressions. He tried not to feel guilty for the way they'd left him. He could picture the Greek's face all red when he discovered them missing.

They caught the metro to the train station and found the ticket counter. Pen stepped up to buy two tickets and froze. "I forgot to bring any money."

He pulled off his backpack and dug through it, coming up with a handful of coins. "Angela's money. We're lucky she gave it to us."

They bought the tickets and hurried to the platform. Their train was one of the last ones leaving the station. Other travelers pushed past them. Despite the late hour, trains were preparing to leave for all parts of Spain and Europe to get their passengers there in the morning hours.

The twins located the train to San Lorenzo, an older model unlike the sleek, superfast trains that crisscrossed the continent. Quin didn't mind, as long as it got them to the monastery.

The conductor took their tickets as the train pulled out of the station. While he scanned them, he gave the twins a curious look. Quin studied the floor. He moved on without asking any questions. Perhaps children there had more freedom, though he suspected the man didn't want to get involved.

The trip lasted just over an hour. The rocking motion of the train put Quin to sleep. When the conductor shook him awake, Pen was snoozing next to him. "Niños, su destino," the man said.

He rubbed his eyes and mumbled thanks, then jostled his sister awake as the train squealed to a stop in front of a much smaller station. The children disembarked onto an outdoor platform instead of the huge indoor station they'd left in Madrid. They stood there, watching the few other passengers step off and immediately walk away. The station was dark and empty since they'd caught the last train of the night.

"Now what?" Quin whispered. "We can't stay here all night."

"Don't whisper. It makes us look suspicious."

He thought two kids alone on a train platform after midnight already looked suspicious, but he didn't say anything. She pulled out her phone and typed in *Monastery*. After a moment of calculating, the map responded with a route. "It looks like the monastery is five kilometers away."

"Three miles? We're going to walk three miles in the dark?"

"And uphill all the way."

"I hope you're joking." Quin groaned.

Pen wasn't.

The GPS map led them down a wrong village street. He stumbled into a trash can and made what felt like every dog in the village bark and sent the twins sprinting away. After this, she had to adjust their route. They twisted back through San Lorenzo's streets with him reasoning this was why paper maps were better and her defending the faulty technology. They were so involved in their argument, they didn't realize they'd finally emerged from the village onto a deserted road. "Look," she gasped.

At the top of one of the highest hills, the monastery shone like a beacon. Warm light poured out of its four towers and beckoned to them. "Finally," Quin said. "Imagine the time we might have saved if we'd just looked up instead of following your phone."

They'd spent the better part of an hour lost. What if Kostas had discovered them missing? Or Professor Flores?

The only light shone out of Pen's phone, which she constantly tapped to help light their path. The monastery popped in and out of view as the road wound around the hill, and when they couldn't see it, the night felt dark indeed. A slight breeze slowly chilled the valley and the dark outlines of the hills of San Lorenzo were the only objects blacker than the road.

Everything inside him screamed to turn around and go back. Why had he ever thought this was a good idea? Only two things kept his feet moving forward: the next train back to Madrid wouldn't arrive until morning and the image of the stone head in Professor Flores' suitcase. They couldn't go back while the professor was around. Despite what anyone else said, Quin knew the man was guilty.

The light clicked off momentarily. When Pen clicked it on, she whispered, "My battery's getting low."

A dog barked somewhere in the town below and he shivered, even though he could still feel heat rising from the sunbaked road. Looking out over the dark hills, he'd never felt so lonely. He inched closer to his sister.

A car engine whined behind them as it labored up the hill.

"Get off the road," Pen whispered. She pushed him sideways. He stumbled into the ditch and she fell on top of him. Gravel dug into his palms and his sister pinned his legs to the ground with her weight. He didn't dare say anything.

The car's headlights lit up the roadway and they ducked down. He held his breath, though part of his brain told him this had nothing to do with whether the occupant could see them. The car crept by and he willed the driver to keep going. Why was it slowing down, anyway? Had they been seen? Finally, the car sped up and disappeared around a bend in the road, its red taillights winking.

"Who's driving up this road so late at night?" Pen whispered.

"Who's walking up it?" He shook gravel out of his hands and pushed her off him so he could stand.

"Do you think it was Kostas?"

He tried to calculate if enough time had passed since they'd left the hotel for their tutor to find a car to drive out to San Lorenzo. He didn't think so.

"Kostas would call us if he knew we were gone. I think it was just someone driving slowly because it's dark."

"You're probably right." He noticed her turn her phone

to silent, in case the man actually did call.

They crept back onto the road and walked cautiously at first, then quicker when the car didn't return. Their breath came in puffs. The closer they got, the higher the hill. Soon, they could see the glowing steeples of the monastery and the warm light hastened their steps.

Finally, they reached the entrance. The light from the monastery towers gave enough illumination for the children to see the shadowy outlines of a humongous structure. He'd been hoping for a small, simple building that was easy to search. They crossed a courtyard paved in stone, walking close to each other. In the middle of the courtyard, they stopped.

"I didn't expect it to be so big," Pen whispered. Stone walls towered on three sides in the familiar square layout.

"It wasn't just a monastery, but the king's palace, too," he said, remembering Kostas' excitement about the history of the place.

"So where do we go?" she asked.

Dong. Dong.

Pen shrieked and grabbed Quin's arm. He gripped back. Then he let go and gave a shaky laugh. "It's the church bell. Two o'clock on the hour."

She giggled nervously and stepped away from him. Both twins gazed up at the church tower from which the last echo of the bell toll receded into the night.

"Someone's still awake in there."

He took a deep breath and nodded. "Let's go see who."

21

The bell tolls emanated from a small chapel on the end of one of the stone buildings. Pen didn't expect the church to be open, but when she pulled on the large iron handle, the heavy wooden door swung toward her. The twins peered inside. A few candles burned at the front of the chapel, illuminating a wooden cross with the figure of Christ on it. The flickering flames didn't provide enough light to see the entire room, only the shape of the pews and shadowy alcoves. Even Christ's face was lost in shadow. Pen was glad about that. She'd never liked the look of pain and resignation on his face when they had to attend chapel at school.

"Should we go in?" She stared at the gloomy corners. Anyone could be lurking there, and they wouldn't know it.

"Well, it's what we came for." He didn't sound too confident.

They tiptoed inside, drawn to the glowing altar like moths. She thought it might be smarter to slip into an alcove and wait in the dark to see if anyone else appeared, perhaps roused by the sound of the door shutting behind them, but after walking from town through the dark, she was glad to be in the light again. The candles flickered so peacefully, she couldn't imagine that anything bad could happen there.

They sat in the first pew, the silence around them so

immense, she thought she could feel time passing. A candle sputtered and hissed, throwing uneven shadows onto the altar. From there, half the Savior's face was illuminated, his mouth drawn and his eyes lifted toward heaven. *Is he looking for a way out*, Pen wondered, *or just waiting for everything to be over?*

She thought of Abuelito in his hospital bed so far away. Why wouldn't he wake up? Was he waiting for them to find the Codex Cardona? Or for their mother to arrive? Or maybe he was just waiting for it to be over, resigned to his fate. Tears flooded her eyes and blurred the candles and cross into a circle of shimmering light. She thought of Kostas' horror when he discovered they were gone. And keeping what she'd known about the codex from Abuelito and La Condesa had been a form of lying. At least, she'd purposefully withheld the truth.

A hard knot twisted together inside her, making her feel sick. Even though she'd told herself they had to keep the website secret to solve the case, she knew it was wrong. And she'd dragged her brother into it, too. She remembered when her parents first told her of their summer plans—ruining her plans so her parents could both do something important to them. She'd wanted to do something important, too. And where had it gotten them? The middle of nowhere in the dark of night?

She had been so certain they would find the codex, she stopped caring if she had to lie to those around her to find it. Was that who she wanted to be?

Pen turned to her brother to apologize for forcing him to go along with her scheme and keep the website from everyone. Quin's eyes were fixed on the figure on the cross and his mouth was hanging open. The light reflected off his glasses, turning his eyes into twin points of light.

At first, she thought he was having his own religious experience. Then he grabbed her arm and pointed.

"Who's that?"

Pen followed the direction of his finger. A figure

stepped out from behind the cross. He was dressed in dark robes, but light glistened off his halo of thinning white hair. His mouth was pressed into a line, like Christ's on the cross, but his eyes weren't looking to heaven—they were staring straight at them. *An angel?* she thought. *Or something darker?* She shivered. Then the figure stepped fully into the candlelight and the twins saw he wore the plain black robes of a monk.

He stepped down from the altar. "You shouldn't be here."

It took her a moment to find her voice. When she did, it came out as a whisper. "I know, it's late and the church isn't open but—"

The monk shook his head and walked to their pew, standing between them and the altar. Both twins jumped up. Quin backpedaled toward the alcove along the side of the chapel, pulling his sister with him.

"That's not what I meant," he said, catching up to them in two swift strides. "I mean you—Penelope and Quintus Grey Reyes—you shouldn't be here."

That stopped them in their tracks.

"How do you know our names?" Pen asked.

The monk's thin lips showed no trace of a smile, but the frown softened. "I know many things about you both. Or at least I did. I've lost touch."

"Lost," Quin murmured.

"You're him," she said. "Abuelito's friend. You're Francisco Rivera."

He nodded, and a faint smile crossed his lips. "Qué buenos amigos we were." Then he frowned. "But that's over now. It must be." He pinched the bridge of his nose. "My only name now is Bernardino."

"But Abuelito's looking for you," Quin protested. "It's the only reason he's still searching for the Codex Cardona. He thought if he found it, he'd find you."

"And he's been hurt," Pen added. "Someone attacked him in his office and took—"

Quin poked her in the back and she stopped. No need to reveal what the thief had taken. Bernardino didn't look surprised at the news. He nodded slowly and studied his shoes—or where his shoes would be if not hidden by his robe.

"You already know about Abuelito." Her anger burned like the candles on the altar.

The monk cleared his throat gently. "I always keep up with Miguel, even if he doesn't know where I am."

"Then you know he's unconscious, too." Quin's accusation echoed off the stone floor and walls. "He might not wake up."

She thought furiously. There was something familiar about Bernardino's face—his pinched nose and thin eyebrows that lay like brush strokes across his forehead. How could he know about Abuelito unless he'd been in Mexico? How did he recognize them if he'd disappeared several years ago?

She stared hard at the monk. The lack of light made his drab clothes even shabbier and washed any color out of his face like an old oil painting in need of restoration. *Color*, she thought. *That's what's missing.* Suddenly, she could picture it—at the zoo, outside the bookshop, in the café. An old man in a red hat, one that covered the ring of white hair but not the thin lips or sad eyes.

"You were there," Pen blurted out. "You pushed Quin down and stole the painting of the quetzal bird."

Bernardino almost laughed. "What a terrible surprise that was when I opened the envelope and found a cheap tourist's painting. I'm sorry for causing you pain. I only wanted to slow you down so you wouldn't follow me." The monk shook his head. "And yet here you are in Spain. You followed me more than I could have imagined." He sighed and turned toward the cross and the unmoving figure on it. The candles burned low. One sputtered and went out.

"But why?" she whispered. "Why did you steal Camila, the tortilla maker, from our grandparents' house? Why did you follow us?

Pain filled the man's face so that it nearly mirrored Christ's on the cross behind him. "I made a mistake by involving Miguel in this mess," he whispered. "I took the tortilla maker to try to make it right. I shouldn't have contacted him again. I should have left the past in the past."

Bernardino stopped speaking and looked away, but not before the candlelight reflected off the tears in his eyes. When he turned back to them, his face was as stone-like as the chapel walls. "I do wish you hadn't found me," he said as softly as a whispered prayer.

He lunged forward. Pen was normally quick on her feet. After all, she played striker for St. Mary's championship soccer team. This time, it felt like cement held her toes to the floor. She opened her mouth to scream. Then she was shoved sideways, hard. She fell into a pew and tumbled to the floor.

Quin stepped in front of her and held his arms out like he was trying to defend the goal instead of defending her from Bernardino. He glanced back at her and the candles reflected off his glasses, making his eyes glow. He opened his mouth and shouted.

"*Run.*"

22

She crashed into the stone statue of a saint. The impact knocked the breath out of her and she collapsed. Seconds felt like hours as she tried to force air into her lungs. *Get up,* she told herself. *Quin's in trouble.* Pen rolled to her knees and crawled between two pews. She felt dizzy and still gasped for air. Through the pain, she heard her brother shouting.

"Leave us alone. All we wanted was to find you. We're not going to tell anyone where you are."

"It's too late," Bernardino said. "You don't have to tell. They probably followed you to me."

She belly-crawled under the pews toward the back of the church. When she reached the last pew, she rolled out and raced to the heavy wooden doors. Her shoulder jarred at the collision and her breath, never quite recovered, whooshed out of her again.

"Let go of me," her brother shrieked behind her. Pen froze halfway through the door. What was she doing abandoning him to a mad monk? She turned back and saw him struggling with Bernardino at the front of the chapel—struggling and losing. The man dragged him up the altar steps like an Aztec priest with his unwilling sacrifice.

"*Quin!*" The scream knifed through her body. The two figures grappled under the cross, halfway in the dark and light. Then Bernardino pulled Quin into the shadows and they both disappeared. "No," Pen shouted. She let go of the door, ready to charge back down the aisle and tackle the traitorous monk.

"Pen," Quin shouted. "Find Kostas. Get help. Get—"

A door slammed somewhere in the dark depths of the church. Her heart felt like it had been torn from her chest and laid bare on the altar. She staggered and grabbed a pew for support. Quin gone? How was this possible? What was happening? She felt the slow tick of time again as she stared at the empty altar and Christ with his upturned eyes, the depths of his pain on his clearly visible face. *His face,* she thought. *How can I see his face?*

She turned to the door. A dark silhouette held it open, illuminated by a bright light shining in from outside. Pen stepped into the light and shaded her eyes. "Who's there?" she called out. "I need help."

The light came not from a lamp but two headlights. A car idled on the gravel pathway outside the church, its light trained squarely on the chapel doors. Part of her wondered who could be there so early in the morning. The other didn't care. Not with her brother in trouble.

The shadow stepped aside, and the headlights shone into her eyes. Bright pinpricks of light danced in front of her. She heard the heavy church door close, but she had to blink several times before she could see again. A figure moved rapidly toward her. She dropped her hand down, hoping—no, praying—to see Kostas standing before her.

"Hello, Pen." A melodic voice greeted her like it was a sunny day and they were two friends bumping into each other shopping.

She stared at the surprise visitor. "What are you doing here?"

Angela smoothed hair from her eyes and stepped closer to her, ignoring the question and asking one of her own.

"Shouldn't we help your brother?"

The hidden door behind the cross banged shut and Quin struggled out of Bernardino's hands. The old monk was stronger than he'd thought, and though he escaped the tight bear hug the man used to drag him out of the chapel, he still clung stubbornly to his backpack. He could shrug off the backpack, but he would lose the Eagle Warrior and all Abuelito's notes.

Bernardino pulled him through a small office lit by a desk lamp. Quin glimpsed notes and a computer on a desk. So much for the idea monks didn't use modern technology. He tugged him through another door into a dark hallway. "We've got to get to them before they do," he said. Quin had no idea who or what the monk was talking about.

"I have to go back." He stopped so suddenly he nearly jerked the backpack from the man's hand. "My sister will be worried. You said you didn't want to harm us. Let me go and I promise we won't bother you again. We won't even tell Abuelito where you are." He realized he was babbling, but his adrenaline was wearing thin, allowing fear to creep in.

The monk clamped a moist hand over his mouth. "Shh. You'll wake the other monks. The last thing we need is more people involved. As for your sister, it's already too late. Didn't you see the lights? They're here. Followed you from the city. Maybe all the way from Mexico."

"Who?" he whispered, but Bernardino didn't answer. He gripped the backpack tighter and propelled him forward. *He's loco,* Quin thought. *Of course he is.* Only a crazy person would pretend to be a monk to hide from—from whom? Who had Pen? Why was it already too late?

The man led him deeper into the monastery. He glimpsed dark rooms and once thought he smelled bread baking. Monks got up early to pray. Was someone already in the kitchen? By the time he'd thought about crying out, they were turning down another hall, this one lined with closed wooden doors. Bernardino stopped at the third door and shoved a key in the lock. The door swung soundlessly forward, and he propelled him into the dark room.

The door closed behind them and Quin felt the release of tension from his backpack. He was free, but he couldn't see anything. He had the sense of enclosed space as Bernardino brushed past him. The monk snapped on a lamp to reveal a tiny room—smaller than Archie's dorm room at MIT—with a simple bed, desk and chair. He was puzzled. Why had the monk brought him there, then released him? Quin stepped back toward the door. He didn't have to remember the way back to the chapel. He would simply make enough noise to wake the sleeping monks. Then he saw the walls of the room and stopped. "Oh," he gasped.

Every inch of wall space was plastered with drawings like the one in his backpack. Some were rendered in pencil, others in ink, and still more in water colors and oil paints. The history of the Aztecs contained in a single monastic cell. Suddenly, he realized who had drawn the sketch of the Eagle Warrior. Bernardino was an artist, and a magnificent one at that. He stepped closer and examined an ink drawing of some Aztec farmers in a field, then scrutinized a watercolor of a quetzal bird similar to the one he'd received in the bookstore. "These are amazing. There must be hundreds of paintings." The papers rose almost to the ceiling of the tiny cell.

The monk sat down at the desk and opened a small laptop computer. He started typing. "Four hundred and thirty of them." He pulled a small flash drive from the computer and then typed a command. Years of peering surreptitiously over his sister's shoulder kicked in. He focused on the question on the screen.

Do you want to permanently delete all data?

Bernardino clicked one button and the laptop buzzed as the deletion program kicked in. Before he could wonder what was going on, the monk turned to him and held out the tiny flash drive. "Hide that somewhere you think it can't be found. If something happens, get it to your grandfather. If he survives, he'll know what to do. If not, and I'm not around either, then perhaps it no longer matters." The old monk shrugged.

Quin reached out and took the drive, confused. "You want me to hide—"

"Yes, and quickly," Bernardino snapped in an un-monk-like manner. "We need to move."

He gripped the flash drive. His mind felt overwhelmed and completely blank at the same time, like the laptop was deleting his brain cells, too. He looked from painting to painting, trying to make some connection between the Codex Cardona and this room. And then he saw him, staring across the room with familiar, fierce eyes. The Eagle Warrior. Suddenly, like an artist finding inspiration, he had it. "These are all pages from the Codex Cardona. You copied them." He drew in a sharp breath. "Which means you've seen the real codex. You have it."

Bernardino paused at the door and turned. His face fell, and he looked less like a crazy kidnapper and more like a tired old man. "Yes," he said, his sadness conveyed in one word. He swept his gaze around the room. "I copied every page. I wanted to remember them exactly the way they were before I sent them away."

Quin stared, too. Before them, over four hundred paintings brought to life a society nearly five hundred years old and long since lost to the world. *Bernardino might be crazy,* he thought, *but he loves art, and Abuelito never gave up searching for him.* If his grandfather trusted him once, maybe Quin could, too.

He found the eyes of the warrior again, an eerie replica to the one hidden inside his backpack. Twins who would never meet. A chill rushed through him. Where was his twin?

Down the hall, a door slammed. Bernardino jumped. "We must go now. Hide the flash drive somewhere safe."

Quin stared at the small black square in his hand.

"Should I put it—"

"Don't tell me." The monk waved the comment off. "Don't tell me where it is or what you do with it. Just get it away from here, like I asked, and maybe someday—" He glanced once more at the paintings. "Maybe someday, these pages will be a book again."

He peered into the hall and Quin stooped and tucked the drive into his shoe. Then, even though Bernardino hissed at him to hurry, he rustled through his backpack. He wouldn't leave Pen on her own. He felt the Eagle Warrior's approval at what he was about to do. When he finished, Quin nodded in respect and ran after the monk.

23

"Penelope, where's Quin?" Angela asked. "Who took him?"

I don't remember telling her my full name, Pen thought. The thought must have shown on her face because the woman said, "I did some digging on you two after our meeting. Hiring a couple of child investigators is a little unusual."

She nodded. How many times had she typed in internet searches on other people? Still, she didn't answer the question. Why was she hiding Bernardino's identity?

The church door opened, and another person walked in. If she had been surprised to see Angela, she wasn't startled to see her companion. In fact, she felt vindicated.

"Of course you're here." She held back none of the venom Abuela had admonished her for. "You've been following us since Mexico. You can't have the Eagle Warrior."

Professor Flores shook his head. "That tongue of yours, Penelope, does not match your pretty face."

She stuck her tongue out and turned to Angela. "What are you doing here? And why did you bring him?" At the same time, her mind raced with thoughts of what could be happening to Quin. Every story she'd ever read about murderers and psychopaths filled her mind with horrifying possibilities.

"After meeting you in the café, I couldn't get the Codex

Cardona out of my mind. Why go so far and give up? So I decided to tell Professor Flores everything."

Pen spared a second to glare at the professor before Angela continued.

"But he had already left Mexico with you two. I took the next flight to Spain, tracked him down, and told him everything—how I borrowed the paintings from him, hired you to find the Codex Cardona, and then warned you not to search anymore."

"You were looking for the codex the whole time, just as I suspected," Professor Flores interrupted, giving Pen a furious look. He took a step closer and she drew back, the incident in the airport fresh in her mind. "You have no idea how dangerous this situation is. I tried to tell your tutor, but he chose to believe you're innocent of any misdoings. As soon as I left your hotel, Angela informed me she'd seen you come out of the alley. More of your investigating, as she calls it."

He pointed a long finger in Pen's face. "You are playing a child's game while real people are getting hurt around you. If it weren't for Angela, nobody would know where you'd gone. What would your mother say?"

Now she did step back, the professor's words as sharp as a slap across her cheek. Her eyes stung, and she drew her breath for a quick retort, then choked it off.

He was right.

Abuelito was in a hospital bed, and she had no idea where her brother was. How could she be so stupid as to imagine herself an international investigator, able to solve mysteries with a little knowledge and flair? So the words she choked out, though not the ones she wanted to say, were the right ones.

"Bernardino took Quin. We have to get him back."

Walking through the silent monastery felt like trespassing on holy ground. Quin tried to tiptoe after the monk, but he'd never been one for stealth and the slap of tennis shoes on tile sounded like crashing waves in the silent hallway. Bernardino rushed ahead, his swishing robes the only indication of his presence. While he followed the monk, he tried to make sense of his situation. This man had forcibly taken him from the chapel. He should stop following him and find someone to help him. He thought if he stopped now, the monk wouldn't come back for him. The man was practically running, and the power of his fear ate at Quin. *He's afraid of whoever's following us. More afraid of them than of me escaping.*

And then there was the flash drive stuck like a pebble inside his shoe. It nestled under the tongue and he had tied his laces extra tight to ensure it wouldn't fall out. *Why did Bernardino give that to me?* Quin wondered as he hobbled down the hall. That, more than anything, propelled him forward instead of making him call for help. They finally exited the building through a side door. The damp, sweet fragrance of flowers greeted them, and the moonlight revealed a garden of trimmed hedges and flowers. They passed a silent fountain of Mary holding baby Jesus. The figures glowed silver in the moonlight. The monk stopped beside the statue and gestured for him to catch up.

"This garden goes all the way up the hillside," he whispered when Quin reached him. He noticed the monk rested one hand on Mary's foot and the other over his heart. He didn't know if he was praying or trying to catch his breath. Maybe both.

"There is a grove of olive trees farther up the hill," the man continued. "It is a wonderful place to hide. Go there now."

"Why? Who's after us? My sister—"

"No time," Bernardino panted. "You must hide what I've given you and yourself so you can go back to your grandfather."

"What about you?"

Bernardino straightened, letting his hands fall to his

sides. "I abandoned my dearest friend to pursue the Codex Cardona alone. I gave in to my own greed and desire and because of this, your grandfather is injured, and you and your sister are in danger."

He dropped his head and drew a deep breath. When he looked up again, his eyes glinted wetly. "Perhaps this is God's justice. My namesake didn't abandon the Aztecs. He stayed with them for sixty years and showed them the love of God. He learned their ways instead of selfishly taking his own path. I'm not worthy of carrying his name."

A light blinked on in a window close by. Bernardino stepped close and grabbed his shoulders. Quin stiffened, still afraid the monk might drag him away, but he whispered, "Go now, and don't come back until I call or you see the police. And don't let anyone find the flash drive, or the codex is lost forever."

"But Pen—"

"I will try to help your sister." The monk released him, physically turned him up the hill, and gave him a light push. Quin took a deep breath and started running.

The candles burned so low they gave only a faint glow. Pen, Angela and Professor Flores hurried to the altar and looked around.

"Quin?" she called out tentatively. Her voice echoed in the nearly empty building like a spirit reaching back across time. She shivered. *Quin's fine*, she told herself, reining in her panic.

"You said he disappeared behind the altar?" The professor didn't wait for her answer but stepped up to the cross, glanced up briefly, then walked around it. He disappeared into the darkness as Quin had.

"There's a door," he called back. Angela grasped Pen's shoulder and they went through the darkness together. Dim lamplight revealed a hidden office—empty—and an open door leading into the monastery.

"I think it's time we wake the monks and call the policia," Professor Flores said.

An ironic statement for someone who'd been detained by the police himself earlier in the day, but Pen didn't disagree.

"That will slow us down," Angela said. "You call the police and Pen and I will continue to search in the meantime."

"This man who took Quin could be dangerous. Pen should stay here with me."

She wavered between holding back and telling the truth, but she remembered her decision to lie had gotten them into this mess. She sighed. "His calls himself Bernardino, but his name is Francisco Rivera."

"Rivera?" His mouth dropped open. "Miguel's friend? The museum director? We thought him dead."

Angela's dark eyes narrowed. "We need to find him now before he disappears again."

Professor Flores shot her a funny look. "What do you know of Francisco Rivera?"

The grad student shook her head, the wrinkle between her eyes fading. "Nothing. I'm merely worried about Quin. We don't want him to disappear, too."

This statement sent Pen's stomach into a rollercoaster of activity. Quin gone forever? She tugged her arm. "You're right. We can't wait. Not if we can help Quin first."

Angela nodded, and they hurried to the door leading into the monastery.

"Wait," Professor Flores called. "I'm calling the police now."

But she didn't stop and neither did her companion. They hurried down the hall. Moonlight fell through a few windows, lighting their way and allowing them to peer into darkened rooms. They contained tables and chairs and a few stiff-backed couches. They found a small dining hall and followed the smell of baking bread to a closed door. A crack of light showed under the door and Pen nearly walked through it, but Angela held her back.

"Shouldn't we ask whoever's inside if they've seen Quin or Bernardino?"

The woman shook her head. "It'll take too long. Let's keep looking on our own."

Reluctantly, she followed the woman down a narrow hallway instead. The doorways were shut, but the sound of snoring reverberated through a few of them. It felt strange to sneak around while people were sleeping. Like a thief in the night. It was exactly the kind of thing she'd imagined when she created the website, but the reality of it was terrifying.

Angela stopped and pointed to a door cracked open enough to allow dim light to filter out. She tiptoed to the door and peeked inside, then pushed the door open. "No one's here."

She stepped inside with Pen close on her heels. They both gaped at the walls covered from floor to ceiling in Aztec art. "I think we're closing in," the woman said. "Let's go."

Pen searched for something that would tell her Quin was okay. She nearly cried out when she saw it but stifled the urge. She stepped closer to the painting to be sure. There was no mistaking the Aztec warrior with the purple head pinned to the wall in the midst of all the others. He'd left the warrior for her. His eyes glowed through the purple wax. *Careful,* they cautioned.

"What is it?" Angela snapped from the doorway.

"Nothing." She decided to keep the warrior to herself. After all, this had been a secret she and her brother shared.

"Then let's go. They're getting away."

Angela hurried down the hallway and she had to run to keep up. The light didn't reach this far, and she could barely see the woman ahead of her. When she stopped, Pen stumbled right into her, knocking the grad student into the door she'd stopped to examine. The door opened, and both girls spilled out into the warm night air scented with roses.

"You clumsy—" Angela started to say.

"Sorry." She scrambled to her feet. "I—" Then, she stopped. A silent figure stood a few feet away, observing them by moonlight. His robes were blacker than the night, which edged toward dawn's grey light now. Next to him, a statue of Mary and her child gazed down on them.

"Come here, Penelope," Bernardino said, his voice soft but urgent.

"Where's my brother?" She stood next to Angela, rooted by indecision.

"He's safe. You're the one in danger."

Angela was on her feet now. She threw a hand in front of Pen. "Don't listen to him." To Bernardino she said, "Where's the codex, Francisco?"

She stared at her companion. "Do you know him?" she whispered. The grad student didn't answer. She kept her eyes on Bernardino. He smiled, and it mirrored the smile of Mary standing over him as she cradled her child. "It's safe, too. Back in the world where it should be."

"You thief," Angela spat. "I've wasted two years tracking you down."

He shrugged. "You can choose to stop anytime."

"You know I can't," Angela replied. "I need the money for my mother." Her voice caught, and she sniffed once.

The monk sighed. "There are other ways to help your mother than working for criminals."

Pen looked from Bernardino to Angela, mystified by this exchange. She didn't know who to trust anymore, except Quin, and he wasn't there. Then she remembered the Aztec warrior in the monk's dorm room. He had been there. He'd pinned the warrior to the wall for her, so he must have followed the monk willingly from the room to the garden.

If he was hiding nearby, she'd never see him through the hedges. *Maybe he just slipped away,* she thought, *and Bernardino has nothing left to bargain with. That's why he wants me.* But then there was Angela showing up in the middle of the night with Professor Flores, and he had Abuelito's stone head. He had to be her grandfather's attacker. Was he calling the police or making sure nobody came to help them?

The monk straightened as if coming to a resolution. He reached out a hand toward Pen. "Niña, I am your Abuelito's oldest friend. Trust me."

She took a step toward him. Angela reached out and grabbed her arm. "Let go. I want to find my brother." She tried to twist away but the woman's grip was surprisingly strong.

"So do I. You're going to help me."

She turned to Angela. Something flashed in the woman's hand, hard metal reflecting the moon's glow.

"Sorry, Penelope," she said. "But you can't be an international investigator and not expect betrayal." She pushed her toward Bernardino and pointed the gun at them both. "Now, let's go find your brother."

24

Quin raced toward the hillside. Soon, he was out of the manicured monastery garden and in an olive grove. He stopped to catch his breath among the squat, gnarled trees and looked back down the hill, but he couldn't see anything except the glow of a window in the monastery.

He turned back to the grove and moved slowly through the trees, imagining the horror of stepping on a snake. Did they come out at night?

Thick leaves blocked the moonlight and he tread carefully through the dark. The branches loomed over him like giant arms, waiting to scoop him up. He shivered and shook his head. Why did he have to have such an overactive imagination? Pen should be there, not him. He needed one of her crazy, ingenious plans. She would never be afraid to march into a dark grove of trees. He sighed. His sister handled these situations better than he did. But she wasn't here.

They're just trees, Quin told himself. He stepped carefully around the thick trunks. Thud. Thud. He jumped and dashed behind the nearest tree. He peered out, but nothing moved, at least nothing he could see. But something was making noise. Footsteps? Had Bernardino caught up to him? Or worse, the people the monk was afraid of?

The wind rustled the leaves. Something hard rapped

him on top of his head. He yelped and dashed away from the tree. His foot caught a tree root and he sprawled forward, hitting the ground hard. He lay still, trying to catch his breath and listen for his attacker. The top of his head stung, but he couldn't find a bump.

Thunk. A tiny missile landed in front of his nose. He scrambled back as his brain registered what it was. He reached forward and scooped up his assailant—a hard, unripe olive.

"Nearly defeated by an olive. Ridiculous." He tossed the fruit away and took a deep breath. Bernardino had asked him to hide. He didn't want whoever was chasing them to know about the codex, which meant Quin didn't want them to, either. At least, not until he learned where the monk had hidden the painted book. He pulled the flash drive out of his shoe and tucked it into his jeans pocket. He'd promised he would hide it. Where was the harm in that?

Quin stood. The trees no longer looked so scary. In fact, their low branches and twisted trunks offered plenty of places to hide. *What would Pen do?* he asked himself. He remembered countless games of hide and seek with his sister in their sprawling home in Boston. She always found the best hiding places, but she could never stay hidden for long. He wondered where she was now. He didn't know who was chasing him, but he had a terrible feeling she did.

Should he hide as Bernardino told him to, or go back for her? He'd always been better at hiding, but what if it put her in more danger? How could he decide? The Eagle Warrior came unbidden into his mind, strong and resolute. Quin felt certain Pen had found the warrior and soon, they would find each other again. Until then, he had to keep the flash drive safe. He started looking for the perfect tree to climb.

Pen was out of ideas. Angela forced them through the garden and up the hill, away from the monastery. The dark shapes of trees dotted the hillside, blocking any view of the top. *Think*, she told herself. She'd always been able to find solutions to her problems, but usually, she had a computer in front of her. A computer couldn't help her now. She stiffened. Or could it?

Their captor had confiscated her bag, but her smartphone was still inside. If she could get her phone, she could open Odyssey. It would pinpoint her location and Archie would know where she was. All she had to do was get the phone.

She thought of the way Quin was able to switch one painting for the other at the bookshop, and how he'd done it again in Bernardino's room. She needed his subtle sleight of hand. Then she realized that if he was with her, Angela would have all she wanted and no reason to keep anyone alive. *I'm on my own,* Pen realized. She couldn't count on Quin to leap in and help her if she carried things too far. That thought sent a double shiver of anxiety and excitement through her.

"Angela," she said loudly. If Quin were nearby, he would hear. "Why are you doing this? I thought you were a graduate student. I thought you loved art."

"Shh," she responded. She motioned for her to keep walking ahead of her. Beside them, Bernardino moved silently but for the rustle of his robe. Something about her question must have bothered her because the woman responded.

"I do love art, or at least, I did." Pen could hear the frown on her face. "I took this job because it was the only way I could afford to pay for medicine for my mother."

"By stealing?" Bernardino jumped in. "By forcing an old man to disappear in order to stay safe?"

She slowed down so she was almost side by side with

Angela instead of walking in front.

"Not stealing. Finding," the woman replied, her voice escalating. "Hardly any different from what you and your brother have been up to." She looked at Pen and she tucked the hand reaching for Angela's bag behind her back.

"It's not the same at all," she said. She couldn't help but be drawn in. "We were looking for the codex to help Abuelito. We wanted to find his friend. We were looking for you," she said to the monk, her voice carrying more accusation than she meant.

"And a good thing you were," Angela said. "You led me right to him. Stumbling onto your website turned out to be the best lead I've had on tracking down Francisco in two years of searching. I'd nearly given up."

Pen felt dismay ripple through her. *Keep talking,* she told herself. "Lucky you. And I thought I was being clever. I guess I'm not as smart as you." She gritted her teeth and reached out. Her hand brushed her bag and she felt for the outside pocket.

"You didn't do so badly. I wouldn't have spotted Francisco in the zoo if we hadn't arranged to meet. I followed him to the bookshop. When he took the painting from Quin, I realized he was my mysterious quarry, and for some reason, he was following you."

Pen's fingers slipped inside the pocket and drew out her phone. She tucked it behind her back, grateful for the darkness. "Yes, if it wasn't for us, you might not have found the codex at all. I guess we are as smart as you."

Angela stopped walking. "Do you know why I met you in the café? To tell you not to pursue this anymore. I didn't want you and Quin getting hurt."

"But you didn't mind hurting Abuelito, did you? You attacked him. He could die." As she said the words, the full impact of this truth hit her for the first time. She might have to live in a world with no Abuelito in it.

"I didn't mean for your grandfather to be badly hurt. I'm not a monster," the woman shouted. She took a deep breath. "And I don't know who Camila is, but I haven't been to your grandparents' home. Now enough of this middle-school banter. Call out to Quin and tell him everything's all right."

Pen shifted the phone to her other hand and slid it around the side of her body until she held it in front of her, shielded from Angela's view.

"Don't do it," Bernardino said. "Quin is safe. The other monks will be up by now. They will discover I am missing at morning prayer and begin a search. If I were you, I would be on my way," he told their captor. As if in response to his words, the church bells began to chime. Their peals filled Pen with hope.

"Quin, it's okay to come out now. We can go back to the monastery and *find Archie*." She opened the Odyssey app as she spoke and typed one word. *Help*. Light resonated from the screen, chasing away the night. She clicked send.

"What are you doing?" Angela shouted. She lunged forward and snatched the phone, the anger on her face clearly visible in the phone's light. She glanced down at the screen and frowned, puzzled. Pen breathed a sigh of relief. Thanks to Archie's self-destructing messages, the phone showed no signs of the message she'd sent.

"I thought Quin would be able to see me," she stammered.

"And me, too," the woman snarled. She turned the phone off and shoved it in her pocket. Then she grabbed her shoulder and yanked her close. Pen gave up all pretense of being obedient. She was no good at it anyway.

"Quin," she screamed. "Don't come down!" Then she clapped a hand over her mouth, realizing her mistake too late. When she'd turned on the phone light, she'd seen one tennis shoe glowing softly in a branch not far away.

Angela shoved her hard, and she would have fallen but Bernardino stepped in and caught her.

"We're done being best friends, Penelope. I'm afraid we're all running out of time," Angela sneered. She waved the gun at them to remind them who was in charge. Then she lifted her voice to the olive trees and shouted, "Quintus, if you want your sister to stay alive, you have five seconds to get out of that tree."

25

Quin picked a tree with a branch low enough to the ground for him to pull himself up easily. He climbed as high as he dared. His movement rained olives to the ground. He hoped the monks wouldn't mind. He settled into the crook of a branch and checked to make sure the flash drive was still in his pocket. That was when he heard voices.

Pen's voice was easy to identify, shrill and loud. The second voice was definitely female and familiar, but he couldn't place it. He leaned over the tree branch he was perched on, straining to hear other voices he might recognize. He hoped for Kostas' deep booming one but instead, he heard the low cadence of Bernardino. *Three people*, he thought. Pen, whom he could trust, Bernardino, who'd charged him to trust no one, and an unknown woman, all coming up the hill toward him.

Quin was out of time to come up with a plan. He shrugged off his backpack and put it carefully on his lap, bracing his back against the V in the tree branch. Now, he needed to hide the flash drive. He unzipped the backpack and stuck his hand inside, searching for something—anything—to hide the drive in. When his hand touched the empty folder that had held the Eagle Warrior, he felt a brief sadness that the warrior wasn't with him.

He found Abuelito's notes, his camera, a sketchpad and

colored pencils, his phone, and one sock. He sniffed the sock. Definitely dirty. He risked turning on the phone, thinking he could call for help. The battery was dead. Why didn't he ever think to charge it? He was stuck with pointed pencils and a smelly sock. Even a good investigator couldn't do much with that.

A light flashed not far from his tree. Quin jerked his feet up and grabbed for a branch, his momentum almost toppling him over. He clutched the branch and stared at the pale light below. His sister's face flowed a strange ghostly white. She had her phone out. Her voice carried through the trees. "We can go back to the monastery and *find Archie.*"

Archie? Their brother was still home in Boston. And wasn't that Angela wrestling the phone away from his sister? What was she doing there, and why was she attacking Pen?

Then he put the words together. *Find Archie!* She had pinged their brother, so Archie would know something was wrong. Relief swelled up in him and he felt he might float out of the tree, but just as quickly, it burst. Archie was half a world away. Even if he understood the message, how could he help?

Then Pen screamed, and Quin forgot everything else. He grabbed the dirty sock and stuffed the flash drive inside, then tied it tightly to a tree branch as high above his head as he dared reach. He jammed the colored pencils in his pockets and looped the camera around his neck. If he were an Eagle Warrior, he'd have a real spear and shield instead of pencils and a camera, he thought. But the flash of light from Pen's phone had given him an idea—the only one he had. He shifted the backpack onto his back and was preparing to climb down as silently as he could when he heard people beneath him. He hadn't been as quiet as he'd thought.

"I hear you," a voice called out. Definitely Angela's. "Let me tell you what's going to happen. If you don't climb down and bring me whatever this monk," she laughed at the word, "foolishly decided to give you, I'll have to hurt your sister. Nobody wants that, Quintus." Something clicked below him. It sounded suspiciously like a gun, or at least the way it sounded in the movies. His sister yelped and then cried out, "Let go."

"I cannot permit you to do this," Bernardino said. "You can't harm these children because of my obsession with the Codex Cardona."

"Then get that boy out of the tree and tell me where you've hidden the painted book. It's as simple as that. Otherwise, I'll start with the girl." Quin couldn't see what she was doing, but he heard Pen yelp again.

"Leave my sister alone."

"Are you going to come down out of that tree and make me?" She actually laughed, and his blood boiled. He'd hoped to be on the ground when he put his plan into action, but this would have to do.

"Look out," he shouted, hoping the woman would look in his direction. Then he picked up his camera and fired off a series of high speed, flash-inducing shots. The light captured movement below like an old movie. Angela shouted and covered her eyes. Bernardino rushed at her and Pen twisted out of her grasp.

He heard shuffling below. "Watch out," his sister shrieked.

"Get off me or—" Angela's threat was cut off.

"Run, niña," the monk shouted.

The roar of the gun blasted Quin's eardrums. He jerked as something crashed through the branches near his head. *Definitely not an olive.* The thought flashed through his mind. His foot slipped off the branch and he fell backwards. He grasped for the tree and rough bark scraped his fingertips as he tried desperately to hold on. The branch slipped through his fingertips and the last thing he heard as he fell through the air was the sound of his sister's scream.

Pen wondered how things could continue to happen around her when she felt frozen in time. Quin's white sneaker slipped off the branch and then his dark shape tumbled to the ground, landing with a sickening thud. She ran to his side, vaguely aware of Bernardino wrestling Angela for the gun. She leaned over him and shook him. "Quin," she shouted loudly enough to wake the entire monastery. "Wake up."

He gasped, then moaned. She felt her heart flop and she struggled to breathe again. Her brother was alive. It was all she needed at that moment.

"Uff." Bernardino landed next to her. He knocked her off balance and she toppled over her brother.

"Ouch," she yelped as something sharp bit into her palm. She shook her hand and felt the object fall out. It hit Quin's chest. She fumbled around for it and found a long, thin item with a pointed end—one of his colored pencils! She grasped the pencil like a spear, ignoring the sharp pulse of pain in her palm.

"You just couldn't go home like I told you to. I told you and Quin to stop looking for the codex. I told you it was too dangerous to continue. Why didn't you listen?"

She stood over them, her arm outstretched. Pen could dimly see the shape of the gun. With Quin injured, she was out of options. She wouldn't abandon him.

"My mother always said I never listen." The words sparked a memory of what Angela told them in the café about her own mother being sick. "Would your mother want you to hurt children to get her medicine?"

"You don't know anything about my mother," she rasped. "Give me the codex. Is it in his backpack?" She stepped closer to the twins.

She hunched over her brother and gripped the pencil tightly. "Don't touch him."

"The codex is not here," Bernardino said softly. "You've

gotten in too deep, Angela. You must let these children go or you'll not be able to come back from this darkness."

"Fine," the woman spat. "They can stay here. You'll go with me to my car." She pointed the gun at Pen. "And you and your brother will not tell the police anything about me. Remember, I know about you. Your grandparents, Archie, Kostas, your parents."

The threat knifed through her. She curled her fingers so tight around the pencil her nails dug into her palm. She ignored the blood oozing from the pencil wound.

"Don't follow us," Angela continued. "Don't look for us, and under no circumstances will you look for the Codex Cardona—or any painted book—ever again."

Angela hauled Bernardino to his feet by his robes. "Forgive me," the monk cried. Pen didn't know if he was speaking to her, or God, or both. "I never meant for this to happen. I only wanted to save what was left of the Aztecs."

His voice grew stronger, ringing out through the trees. "I wanted to preserve what my ancestor worked so hard to create. I wanted to save the codex page by page and deliver it to every museum in the world for everyone to see."

"Quiet," the woman said. "Or I'll change my mind about the children." She turned back to the twins. "One more thing. Give me the camera. I can't leave you with evidence."

Pen knew if she was going to act, it had to be now, but she felt as if a spell had turned her into stone. If Angela walked away, she would always fear for her family. She could imagine the nightmares in the days ahead, wondering if she would return to make sure the twins never spoke of the codex. Or she might hurt Abuelito again, or Kostas, or Mamá. The possibilities were endless. They held her frozen in a web of terror. She shut her eyes and wished she'd never thought of the website or being international agents.

Her brother groaned but managed to sit up beside her. "You want my camera? Come and get it." She cringed at the pain in his voice, but at the same time, pride filled her.

When had her brother gotten so brave?

"Ready?" he whispered. She started, then realized he knew what she held in her hand. Pen swallowed hard. She wasn't an Eagle warrior, but she could defend her family like one.

Quin struggled to his feet, groaning. Pen wasn't sure what he'd injured, but it must be bad. She reached out to steady him. He raised his arm, and she glimpsed his camera in his hand. He was taking a picture? Now? Then it came to her what her brother was doing. Creating a distraction.

"Say cheese," he shouted.

She dove forward like a soccer star leaping for a diving header. She drove the pencil spear-like down, down, finding nothing but air. She despaired, mid-leap. She'd missed her mark. Then, just as she hit the ground, the pencil's tip collided with a solid body.

Angela's scream pierced the night air. "My foot." She collapsed to the ground and moaned in pain. Pen scrambled away, winded, but triumphant. That would teach Angela to wear high heels again. Her head spun, and her legs could no longer hold her. She sank down next to Quin and grabbed his hand. He squeezed back. Angela moaned and limped to them.

"I gave you a chance," she gasped, her words punctuated by a grunt of pain. "I am done with you both."

She gripped her brother's hand harder and closed her eyes, glad they were together. *If we ever get home,* she thought, *I will never try to solve a mystery again.*

The night exploded with noise. She opened her eyes in time to see a dark shape hurtle into Angela and tug the gun away. All around them, shouts of "policia" broke the silence. A dozen or more shadows rushed toward them, chasing the last of the darkness away with their flashlights.

"Pen?" Quin mumbled, his voice low. "Estás bien?"

Her brother must have hit his head if he was speaking Spanish to her. "Sí." She squeezed his hand. "Everything's okay."

"Argh," he said. "Let go of me. I think I broke my arm."

She felt someone kneel next to her and grab her shoulders. The same person who had hurtled into Angela. "Penelope and Quintus Grey Reyes, I've been looking everywhere for you."

Pen felt her eyes fill with tears. She'd never been so happy to see Professor Flores.

26

From the hospital in the village, Quin could see the road to the monastery and the hills and olive trees. He turned away from the window and shifted in the bed, trying to ignore the dull pain in his arm and the sharp pricks along his backside. Unfortunately, he'd broken all but one of his pencils in his fall. The doctor asked if he'd been attacked by a colorful porcupine. Quin hadn't found that funny. He wouldn't be able to sit normally for a week, and with his broken arm, he couldn't draw or paint for the rest of the summer.

He was looking out the window because it was easier than looking at the rest of the people in his hospital room. Adam Grey had arrived that morning looking so faint the nurse had promptly taken his pulse and told him to sit down. He couldn't seem to say more than, "You did what? But how did...I mean, why would you—" as Pen related the entire story, starting with the creation of their website.

Kostas had no such difficulty finding words, but in his fury, he slipped into Greek occasionally punctuated by Latin. Professor Flores said nothing, and as soon as Adam Grey arrived, he slipped out of the hospital room.

Pen finished telling them how Quin had fallen from the tree and how she'd grabbed his pencil—the only one still intact, as it turned out—and punctured Angela's foot so the former grad student couldn't run away.

At this, the tutor stopped speaking Greek and raised his bushy eyebrows at her. "Her foot? Like Achilles?"

Her face turned red, but she nodded. Kostas cocked his head and wrinkled his brow. "My Gemeni do listen to my stories." He leaned back in the hospital chair and crossed his arms over his large chest. Quin couldn't be sure, but he thought the man might be fighting a smile.

A police officer walked in to take their statements again. "Have you found Bernardino—I mean Franscisco, yet?" Quin asked.

After the chaos settled down and the police arrested Angela and rushed Quin to the hospital, they discovered Bernardino was missing. The police would probably arrest him, Adam Grey explained, if they thought he'd carried stolen art across international borders.

"No," the officer said. "His room was completely empty. No drawings, no computer."

He opened his mouth to insist the room had been full of paintings, but the officer waved him off. "But we found this with your name on it." He walked to the bed and held out a scroll of dark paper. Quin grabbed it and unrolled it, his heart in his chest. When he saw the Eagle Warrior's familiar face, purple crayon and all, he smiled. Though the warrior's face remained the same, in his eyes, he saw fierce pride. A small note fell onto the sheets.

Found this among my things. I wish to return the art to its original owner. Perhaps you and your sister could help. Good luck.

"Good luck?" Adam Grey asked, reading the note from the other side of the bed. "What does he mean?"

Quin shrugged and rolled the painting up carefully, shooting his sister a "let's talk later" look. The nurse walked in and frowned at the full room. "Fuera. Out. Let this boy rest." The policeman, Kostas, and Adam Grey exited. Pen paused at the door and bit her lip, her eyes suddenly large.

He waved before she said anything. "I know. I'm glad you're okay, too. Don't forget to do that thing I asked you to do." He glanced behind her to make sure Kostas or their father hadn't heard.

She grinned and whispered, "You better tell me what you're hiding about Bernardino and the codex soon." When she popped out the door, he leaned back against the pillows, exhausted, but the night's events still whirled in his head. When he thought about all the things that could have gone wrong, and what could have happened to him and his sister, he shivered.

The investigation had started as a fun way to spend the summer and gotten so out of control, Quin suspected even Pen felt taken aback. Even though he knew they were both lucky Professor Flores had called the police and Bernardino had helped them escape Angela, a part of him felt proud of the role he'd played in her capture. The police told him his photos would be used as evidence and had praised him for his quick thinking. Even Pen had been impressed, he could tell.

The world started to go fuzzy as the pain medication kicked in. He unscrolled the Eagle Warrior and propped him up on the bedside table. The warrior lifted his spear in a salute before dropping back into his normal pose. "It's the medicine," he mumbled to himself. Still, he lifted his good arm and waved back. The last thought he had before he drifted to sleep was to ask the Eagle Warrior to go wake up Abuelito.

With Quin at the hospital, Pen had to do all the explaining to Mamá. She wished for once her family wasn't so fond of using the webcam. Her mother's beautiful features were drawn and her usually bright eyes darkened by concern and circles of fatigue.

"Ay, m'ija," Mamá said when she finished telling her story, or at least most of it, "Porque no confias en mi?"

The words struck her hard. Why couldn't she confide in her mother? She opened her mouth to tell her she did but stopped. Instead, her eyes filled with tears she tried to brush away before the camera could catch them. "It's not easy when you're gone all the time."

Now, Mamá's eyes filled and she didn't wipe the tears away. "When I get home, we will have a long talk, hija, about anything you want."

Pen nodded, not sure how she felt about that. She did want her mother's attention, but closer scrutiny might mean less time to explore things on her own and with Quin. Her thoughts had taken her far away and when she started listening again, Mamá was saying, "The good news is the doctor thinks Abuelito is close to being better. It's true he's not awake yet, but there are signs he could wake up at any moment. It gives me and your Abuela hope."

After saying goodbye, she sat back in the hard desk chair in the hotel room and clasped her hands together. She thought of her grandfather's smile and the way the Eagle Warrior had communicated with her and Quin throughout their search, and how the candles had glowed beneath the cross in the church, and how, just at the right moment, Professor Flores and the policía had found them.

Somehow, they were all connected to the Codex Cardona, to the missing pages, to Bernardino and Abuelito, and to the real Bernardino de Sahagún, the monk who'd left his own country to spend fifty years with people like Camila and the Eagle Warrior. If he could give up his life for another people, surely she could give up one summer to be with her grandparents.

Pen climbed into bed and listened to the rumble of her father and Kostas' voices next door as they discussed travel plans. She was nearly asleep when her phone dinged. She rolled over and automatically picked it up. For the first time, Odyssey didn't disclose Archie's location. She

wondered if there was something wrong with the pro-
gramming.

α: Not spying on anyone, r u?

π: Trying to sleep. Where r u?

α: Top secret mission.

π: I think I've had enough of those for a while.

α: Good! Now buenas noches, mi hermanita.

π: Buenas noches. And thanks, hermano.

She smiled and fell asleep with the phone next to her on
the pillow.

The next morning, the door to Quin's hospital room swung
open and he looked up from a mouthful of tortilla de
patata, expecting to see Pen or his father. Instead, Professor Flores stepped into the room. He cleared his throat.

"Can we talk?"

He swallowed the bland potato omelet and shrugged,
then grunted at the pain the movement produced.

The professor gestured to the cast on his arm. "My con-
dolences."

He thought about saying he wasn't dead, it was just a
broken arm, but he held his tongue. The man was trying to
be nice. Maybe, Quin thought, he just didn't know how to
talk to kids.

"Thanks." He settled back on the pillow and stared at
the professor until the man quit fidgeting and met his gaze.

"I owe you many apologies," Professor Flores began, his
voice hesitant. Quin bet the professor was unused to apologizing.

"I suspected something was not right in Mexico City. I
shared my concerns with your grandfather, but I said
nothing to your mother or grandmother. I thought the risk
was only to myself, and also that if you had your grandfather's painting, as I suspected, it would be a simple matter
to retrieve it, and you would not be in danger. I was
wrong." He cleared his throat again and looked like he'd

swallowed a bite of Quin's breakfast.

Good thing Pen's not here yet, he thought. *She'd make this much harder for Professor Flores.*

"Okay. But in the airport, when you, you know, attacked us—"

The man's face flushed. "Yes," he stammered. "Forgive me for that, too. I desperately wanted the painting back because of the danger and...well, I'd begun to think of it as mine."

"How did you get the Eagle Warrior?"

Professor Flores almost smiled. "He was waiting for me one day on my desk in my office. The envelope had no name on it, but I assumed it was left for me and when I opened it—" He stopped speaking and ran a hand through his greasy hair before wiping the hand on his shirt. "It sounds loco, but I felt like the warrior was asking—no, not asking, demanding—help."

Quin nodded. It didn't sound crazy at all.

"I contacted your grandfather immediately," the professor continued. "I'm the one who got him involved in the search for the Codex Cardona again. Then the warrior disappeared from my office. I assumed it'd been stolen, but I never thought Angela took it. I knew her mother was unwell and in need of costly treatment, but to steal this priceless art..." He fell silent for a moment and stared out the window. "She was my best student."

Quin let this information sink in. "But what about the stone head? The one from Abuelito's desk?"

The professor shook his head. "What about it?"

"You took it," he accused, surprised at how possessive he felt of both the Eagle warrior and the stone head. "I thought you used it to—" He stopped short of accusing him of hitting his grandfather over the head.

Professor Flores shook his head like he guessed his meaning. "Your grandfather was angry when I brought up the subject of the Codex Cardona with him. He said the painted book had been nothing but trouble, and he'd already lost one friend over it. He offered me the stone head and said if I wanted to delve into a mystery, I could research the stone heads, since little is known about them." He shrugged. "Miguel was protecting me. I knew he would look into the codex without me, especially if there was hope we might find Francisco."

"Hmm," Quin said. The explanation made sense. The professor rubbed his hands and stepped closer.

"I talked to the police after Angela was arrested. They have been able to connect her to a larger string of art robberies, one in my own home last year—the same painting I showed off to her one night when she came for dinner. That should have been a clue to me." He frowned and stared at the tile floor.

"Well," Quin said lightly. "We can't all be international investigators."

Professor Flores looked up like he thought he was making fun of him. To his surprise, he laughed. "No," the professor agreed. "Gracias a Dios, no."

27

Pen paused at the sound of voices inside Quin's room. She wasn't eavesdropping, of course, merely analyzing the cadence of voices to see if she recognized them. Of course she did. Professor Flores' voice was so smooth she would know it anywhere. She wondered if Archie could build a program with voice recognition software for her so she could avoid walking into a room full of people she didn't want to talk to. Maybe they could design it together.

The professor came out of the door and she hopped back, trying to look innocent. He frowned but only said, "Buenos dias," and continued down the hospital hallway. They held an unspoken truce between them now. They had all fallen for Angela's ploy.

She thought with a little regret how much she'd liked the grad student. Art thief, she reminded herself. The woman had used being a graduate art student as a cover. Did everyone hold the ability to be more than one person inside them? Could she, Pen, be a thief, or worse? She remembered the way she'd skirted the truth to get her and Quin into some sticky situations. What would she do if he or Archie or Mamá needed help?

She pushed the door open, still deep in thought.

"Finally," Quin shouted at her. "Did you get it?"

"Shh. You want everyone to hear?" She stuck her head

out the door, then closed it and slid a chair in front. She reached into her jeans pocket and pulled out a sock.

"You found it."

She held the sock at arm's length. "Really, Quin? A dirty one?" She wrinkled her nose and reached inside, screwing her face up like it was the most disgusting thing she'd ever done.

"Pen!" he shouted. He pulled himself all the way up with his good arm and grabbed the pillow, ready to wallop her.

"Okay, tranquilo." Pen laughed. She peeled the sock off slowly and held out her hand, bunched into a fist. Then she turned her hand over and opened it, revealing the small flash drive. She shoved the drive at him and produced her laptop from her bag, grateful Kostas had thought to bring it from Madrid.

"You didn't already look? he asked.

"Of course not. It was hard enough sneaking out this morning and hiking to the monastery and back without anyone knowing." She popped the flash drive into a port. They waited anxiously until a file menu appeared with only one folder.

"This is it," Quin whispered. "I think we're about to find the codex after all."

Pen didn't say anything. After all they'd been through with the website, Abuelito's attack, and almost losing Quin, she'd given up hope of ever solving the mystery of the painted book. She clicked to open the folder.

Both twins studied the plain document before them. "It's a list of addresses." She couldn't keep the disappointment out of her voice, not sure what she'd expected—a puzzle, or maybe the secret location of the actual codex.

He pointed to the screen with his one good hand. "Some of these are museums."

She scanned them. "Here's one in Japan and one in Iceland."

"And here's Abuelito's," Quin added. "Why did

Bernardino list all these places?"

Pen chewed her lower lip and stared out the window. On the street below, cars, bicycles and pedestrians all buzzed through the warm Spanish sun.

"What was it Bernardino said right before I attacked Angela?"

Her brother shook his head. "Something about museums but—" He raised his cast. "I was a little distracted by, oh, pain and imminent death and all."

She rolled her eyes. "It wasn't that serious." He raised his eyebrows, ready to protest, so she hurried on. "You're right about the museum part. He said—" She closed her eyes and tried to remember. "Oh." Pen started leaping up and down, jarring his bed.

"Ouch, cut it out. What is it?"

"I know where the Codex Cardona is." She spun in a circle before going on. "Bernardino told us. He told Angela, too. You probably don't remember because you'd just fallen out of that tree and—"

He glowered at her and she hurried on. "Bernardino said he wanted to save the codex page by page and deliver it to every museum in the world for everyone to see."

"Fat chance. We don't even know where he's gone."

"It doesn't matter." Pen pointed to the list. "He's already done it."

Quin scanned the words on the screen. His eyes widened. "You mean he sent a page of the codex to all these places?"

"That's how Abuelito got Camila. Bernardino sent her."

"And how Professor Flores got the Eagle Warrior before Angela stole it off his desk," he added.

"But why?" she asked. "If Bernardino worked so hard to find the codex, why take it apart page by page?"

He scratched his arm at the top of the cast where it itched. "It was safer. Angela could only steal one page at a time that way, and she didn't know where Bernardino sent the pages. Only he did."

"And now us," Pen said thoughtfully.

The door rattled against the chair. She pocketed the flash drive and snapped the laptop shut just as Adam Grey pushed through the door. He maneuvered the chair out of the way to get through and peered at them over the rims of his glasses. "Not done snooping after everything that's happened?"

The twins shared a guilty look. Two international investigators caught red-handed. Then they burst out laughing.

"Never mind," their father said. "I have great news. Abuelito is awake."

$$\mathcal{Q}$$

At first, Adam Grey wanted the children to return to Boston with him, where Mamá would meet them as soon as Abuelito was feeling better. Both twins protested. "It takes so long to get a fellowship with CERN," Quin said. "You should finish it, Dad."

"And Mamá should finish her lectures and promoting her new book," Pen added.

He frowned at them. "So what do you suggest we do with you two?"

"We should go back to Mexico," they both said at the same time. She reached out to pinch her brother's good arm, but he knocked her hand away.

Their father clapped a hand to his forehead. "You didn't even want to be there at all this summer."

Quin grinned, and Pen looked sheepish. "We changed our minds."

After hugging Kostas goodbye and extracting a promise to visit once he was off his crutches, they and their father flew to Mexico City. They even had the same flight attendant. Pen felt, somehow, that this Camila was sent as a sign from the tortilla maker in the painting to reassure her that she was all right, wherever the painting was now.

They arrived at their grandparents' casa that evening, expecting an empty house, but lights shone from the windows. When they knocked on the door, Mamá opened it and threw her arms wide. "Mis hijos." She hugged them tightly before they could even go inside. She kissed both their faces and Pen wiped away a wet mark from her tears.

"Mamá," Quin complained, "you're hurting my arm."

"Ay." Mamá stepped back and let them inside. "I'm so glad you're all safe." She shut the door firmly. "And we'll talk later about everything that happened, including all the things you neglected to tell me and your father."

She gave the twins her best no-nonsense look and they nodded. "But now," Mamá continued, "there are a few people who want to see you."

They walked down the hall to the outdoor atrium. "Oh," Pen gasped. Someone had strung sparkling gold lights from the walls and they twinkled over their heads.

"Es una fiesta," Abuela cried, kissing both twins on each cheek. "And a welcome home party."

She stepped away and the twins saw their grandfather sitting in a wheelchair at the outdoor table. He gave them a small smile and a wave. "Abuelito," they both cried and ran to him.

"Cuidado," he warned the twins as they leaned over and hugged him. "The doctor didn't want to let me go, but La Condesa insisted." He gave their grandmother an admiring glance. From the doorway where she spoke with their parents, Abuela smiled back.

"Abuelito," Pen whispered. "About the codex—"

"And your friend, Bernardino—I mean Francisco," Quin added. "We think we found—"

But the old man raised his hand and stopped them. "Do you remember what I told you when I gave you my notes?"

She shook her head, but her brother said, "You said maybe it was better if we left the Codex Cardona in the past."

Abuelito nodded. "Exactemente." He sighed deeply and patted Quin's cast lightly.

"But you gave us your notes," Pen persisted. "And we

found Francisco. We know where the other pages are."

"And I don't think the curse is real anymore," her brother added. "I think the book just wants to be found by the right people." He hesitated, then added, "People who want to honor the Aztecs for who they were, like Bernardino de Sahagun did, even if they made mistakes, like sacrificing people."

"And the monks made mistakes," Pen said. "Like forcing people to convert to their religion. "Maybe we all make mistakes," she added, thinking about Angela. "And we just need someone else to help us see things differently, like Bernardino de Sahagun tried to do when he sent his painted books to Spain."

Abuelito's smile filled his face. "I'm glad to hear you speak of such things." He gazed past the twins to where their parents and Abuela talked in a huddle. He gestured at Quin's arm and his wheelchair. "But sometimes it's better for mysteries to stay mysteries. Do you understand, mis hijos?"

He held their gazes, his eyes darkened by fatigue but with the same spark inside they always had.

Pen thought of how they'd received help finding the codex in so many surprising ways, and how much could have gone wrong the night at the monastery but didn't. She glanced at her twin, his arm bulky in its cast. Was he thinking about it too? But his eyes looked fierce. In fact, they reminded her of the Eagle Warrior.

They both nodded. "We understand."

Abuelito squeezed each of their hands. "Muy bien."

"Oye," Abuela called as she crossed the courtyard. "You're not sharing secrets again, are you?"

Pen, Quin, and Abuelito shared a smile. "No, mi amor," the old man said. "We're merely discussing how much longer we must wait for dinner." La Condesa launched into a loud protest that she hadn't had time to even think about eating since he had been in the hospital and that their tacos were on the way by special delivery.

Then the food arrived, and the delivery boy turned out to be Archie. He hugged his sister extra hard and whispered, "I have news about Odyssey. I have a buyer for the app. He thinks it will be a great way for parents to keep track of their children." Archie shook his head at this and her cheeks warmed. The thought of her parents using Odyssey horrified her.

"Don't worry," he said. "I'm already working on something else for us to use."

She grinned and hugged her older brother hard. "So that's your big secret?"

Archie nodded. "I didn't want to tell anyone until I knew for sure. I had to fly to California, so I turned the locator off. We're just lucky I didn't do that before you pinged me from San Lorenzo."

Pen nodded, suddenly solemn. *Another thing that could so easily have gone wrong but didn't,* she thought. When Archie received the message she'd sent from the olive grove, he'd immediately called Kostas, who'd called the police, though it turned out Professor Flores had already alerted them. The tutor had gotten to them in under an hour and been a strong, steady presence while they waited for Quin's arm to be set and the pencils removed from his backside. Was it possible for such a series of small coincidences to fall randomly into place, or was this another sign of something much larger?

She tucked her thoughts about coincidence and the universe away for later.

Archie punched Quin in his good arm and promised them both a good older brother lecture after they'd eaten all the tacos. Then the Grey Reyes family enjoyed a rare fiesta in celebration of all that had looked lost and been found.

Pen thought about all the pages in the codex spread out across the world. They hadn't been entirely successful in solving their first case, but they knew where the pages were, even if the Codex Cardona was no longer a book.

Maybe someday, they could track down each page and put the painted book together again.

Until then, it would remain a mystery hidden in the plain sight of the whole world.

Hidden except for those who truly wished to see.

About the Author

Kimberly S. Mitchell loves journeys, real or imagined. She has traveled to five continents and over twenty countries, always with a book in hand (or backpack). Now she writes adventures to send her characters on journeys, too. She lives on a small farm in Northwest Arkansas with her husband, daughters and too many animals to count. Find out more at kimberlymitchell.us.

Acknowledgements

Thank you first of all to you, dear reader. I hope you've enjoyed Pen and Quin's adventure and choose to tell another about the story. The best books are always those recommended by a friend.

Thank you, Gayle and Gary for always believing in me. Thank you, David for allowing me the time and space to write and for being my continual support. Thank you, Jennifer, Lindsay, and Natalie for providing inspiration for the sibling rivalry within the Grey Reyes family and for our own adventures! Thank you to my extended family for putting up with the crazy writer.

Georgia, Cheryl and Matthew, thank you for all those hours spent around the table with a pen and a cup of coffee.

My gratitude to Arnold J. Bauer and his book *The Search for the Codex Cardona* for inspiring me to write about this mysterious painted book.

I'm grateful to Vinspire Publishing for bringing the story of Pen and Quin to life.

Trademarks

The author gratefully acknowledges the use of the following trademark:

New England Revolution soccer jersey.
(REGISTRANT) MAJOR LEAGUE PROFESSIONAL SOCCER, INC. CORPORATION DELAWARE 2029 CENTURY PARK EAST SUITE 400 LOS ANGELES CALIFORNIA 90067

Dear Reader,

If you enjoyed reading the first book in Pen & Quin's adventures, I would appreciate it if you would help others enjoy this book, too. Here are some of the ways you can help spread the word:

Lend it. This book is lending enabled so please share it with a friend.

Recommend it. Help other readers find this book by recommending it to friends, readers' groups, book clubs, and discussion forums.

Share it. Let other readers know you've read the book by positing a note to your social media account and/or your Goodreads account.

Review it. Please tell others why you liked this book by reviewing it on your favorite ebook site.

Everything you do to help others learn about my book is greatly appreciated!

Kimberly Mitchell

PLAN YOUR NEXT ESCAPE!

What's Your Reading Pleasure?

Whether it's captivating historical romance, intriguing mysteries, young adult romance, illustrated children's books, or uplifting love stories, Vinspire Publishing has the adventure for you!

For a complete listing of books available, visit our website at www.vinspirepublishing.com.

Like us on Facebook at
www.facebook.com/VinspirePublishing

Follow us on Twitter at
www.twitter.com/vinspire2004

and follow our blog for details of our upcoming releases, giveaways, author insights, and more!

www.vinspirepublishingblog.com

We are your travel guide to your next adventure!

CPSIA information can be obtained
at www.ICGtesting.com
Printed in the USA
BVHW071239060519
547457BV00010B/1436/P